Matisse:
The Only Blue

GUERNICA WORLD EDITIONS 53

LAURA MARELLO

MATISSE: THE ONLY BLUE

TORONTO—CHICAGO—BUFFALO—LANCASTER (U.K.)
2022

Guernica Editions Founder: Antonio D'Alfonso

Michael Mirolla, general editor
Scott Walker, editor
Interior and cover design: Errol F. Richardson

Guernica Editions Inc.
287 Templemead Drive, Hamilton (ON), Canada L8W 2W4
2250 Military Road, Tonawanda, N.Y. 14150-6000 U.S.A.
www.guernicaeditions.com

Distributors:
Independent Publishers Group (IPG)
600 North Pulaski Road, Chicago IL 60624
University of Toronto Press Distribution (UTP)
5201 Dufferin Street, Toronto (ON), Canada M3H 5T8
Gazelle Book Services, White Cross Mills
High Town, Lancaster LA1 4XS U.K.

First edition.
Printed in Canada.

Legal Deposit—Third Quarter
Library of Congress Catalog Card Number: 2022934030
Library and Archives Canada Cataloguing in Publication
Title: Matisse : the only blue / Laura Marello.
Names: Marello, Laura, author.
Series: Guernica world editions ; 53.
Description: Series statement: Guernica world editions ; 53
Identifiers: Canadiana (print) 20220186391 | Canadiana (ebook) 20220186456 | ISBN
9781771837446 (softcover) | ISBN 9781771837453 (EPUB)
Classification: LCC PS3613.A7397 M38 2022 | DDC 813/.6—dc23

to all the gods, honey …
to the mistress of the labyrinth – honey
—from a Linear B inscription at Knossos

So liberty is really the impossibility
of following the path which everyone usually takes
and following the one your talents make you take.
—Henri Matisse

This book is an exploration of Matisse's work and life, with a focus on his time in Nice.

Contents

Part One:
Distill to Essence   3

Part Two:
Purify the Line   33

Part Three:
Saturate Color   69

Part Four:
Synthesize Line and Color   95

PART ONE:
DISTILL TO ESSENCE

Always a Window

Always a view of a village facing the sea, always a white table, with a blue and green-leafed tablecloth and a gray-blue bowl of orange-flecked-red goldfish.

A village facing the sea: a village facing south to the Mediterranean. The wavy windows glint at midday. Each window has cornflower-blue shutters, a window box with red geraniums, or an ironwork rail protecting a faux terrace, and the geraniums in curvy terracotta pots. The peachy brown of the terracotta and the curvy woman shapes make you want to lie on the beach in the sun, make you want to lie with a woman on a bed, with the second story windows open, with the sun and air coming in, the sounds of people arguing on the street below, bargaining for tomatoes or love, while just out of reach, in secret, you have that love, and you are holding her in your arms, stroking her long blond hair.

A window overlooking every sort of world: beach resort, Nice; Moroccan village, Tangier; hill country, Provence; Paris.

Nothing is Real

The world is too real, so nothing in the paintings are real enough to be real, to be felt as real.

Portraits of Women

Whether languid or frigid, hatless or hatted, whether reclined, seated or standing, in the window or against the draped florid, patterned wall, on the bed or on the chair – they all stare at the viewer. The viewer stares back.

You are not a woman, but you are not a man either. You are genderless. But everyone else has a gender, so why don't you? Men see you as a woman, something mysterious, and women see you as a kindred spirit. But you see women as mysterious, men as strange, and yourself as distant but oddly familiar.

Portraits of women are portraits of the studio, and therefore self-portraits.

Rugs, drapes, paisleys, stripes, easels, sofas, a window, a table, a bowl of fruit, other Matisse paintings hanging tiny and square on the walls, like postage stamps.

Leaves Falling

Regardless of the season, there are no seasons, only summer, only the bright primary colors of hot and wet, of beach and sea, of women and men.

Sailboats on the Bay

Framed by the window, seen through the window, with mauve and lavender right wall, not found in nature, hunter green reflection in the glass, and a coral one below, not found in nature, but echoing the mottled indigo and orange windowsill plants. Boat masts orange against a pink sky striped in lavender, again not found in nature, indigo hulls against a pink and coral, orange bay.

With Signac now, in Saint Tropez, 1904, the light changes. The ocean changes everything. No longer land-locked, the bright colors begin; the art begins. The mystery cracks open and falls, sun bleached starfish*, into your lap. Cry for joy. Cry for loss, loss of family, loss of stability, loss of respectability, loss of the normal bourgeois life. Leave it behind. Step into mystery....

Collioure, 1905

Here your *Matisse palette* emerges in its full brilliance, a year after St. Tropez's revelations, another year, another summer, again on the Mediterranean, now with Derain, the sun is even brighter, the colors even more brilliant, the sky breaks open even further, starfish falling everywhere, immersed in the mystery but not drowning, submerged but not drowning, risky, risky.

Portrait of Derain

His face shaded in ice blue – background in a slightly darker soft blue, so he does his portrait.

Collioure Valley

Collioure mountains – all seen as if through a window, painting a window to create a colored world; then the joy comes into it, the sensuality, the meadows or forest clearings with human bodies grouped together in play, *Collioure luxe, joi* and *volupté; luxe, Bonheur and volupté*; the dancing again. The dance.

Everyone went to Collioure. Picasso went. Derain went. The Fauves and Impressionists.

Wife, and Daughter

Sent back to Paris, *Woman with a Hat* slashed at its first exhibit. 1905. Suddenly you are Fauves. You, who hate naming, have been named. Vauxcelles has named you. Bold. Undisguised. Wild – wildness, certainly, for there must be some wildness, for art to happen, but beasts?

Gertrude and her brothers are buying your paintings, and you are attending her salon. Gertrude tells her companion Alice that she is sitting under the correct painting indeed, the *Woman in a Hat*, who is causing all the controversy. And why is that? Because her face is three shades of blue-green, teal green, sea green, darker for shading? With some pink for contrast? Because she does not look real? This is not a pipe. Because she looks forlorn, almost stern, out at the viewer? Why are they angry?

Everyone is laughing after Gertrude Stein makes her remark, but Alice knows they are not laughing at her, they are applauding her good taste, her choice, and Gertrude is punctuating that choice with her good joke.

In 1910, when Leo and Gertrude split the collection, Gertrude will choose the Picassos and Leo will take your paintings. She will also choose Hemingway, in the Hemingway / Sherwood Anderson rivalry, and she will be wrong again. She will choose Gertrude Stein in the Stein / Hemingway argument, and she will be wrong again. When she chooses Fernande in the Fernande / Marie Laurencin argument, she will still be wrong. She will even be wrong when she chooses scrambled eggs in the scrambled eggs / omelet imbroglio for your "Matisse must be shown he insulted us" lunch.

But when she chose Alice in the Leo / Alice argument, she was right to begin with. And when, before that, she chose Paris in the Paris / Baltimore conundrum, she was right again. And when she chose writing in the writing / medicine imbroglio, she was right again. So, you see, you can be right most of the time to begin with, and then you can go on to be wrong all the time.

The Riverbank, 1907

So many purples: a mauve path along the river, a lavender sky, a purple swath of water where brown branches are reflected. Purple riverbank, the mauves, lavenders and purples you see when you shut your eyes.

In contrast, citrine grass and distant trees, dark moss green leaves of a foreground branch. The N is green: moss or citrine, or sea-foam tree leaves at the top right. The C is the purple, mauve and lavender. The A is the brown branches.

Harmony in Red, 1908

There is no harmony here. It's a dining room as lava pit. The entire space is suppurating the deepest carmine red.

The indigo blue scrolls on the red tablecloth are tentacles searching for the lemons and oranges scattered on the table. The indigo blue scrolls on the red wall reach for the sad, silent, sitting woman herself, who is absent, vacant almost, not really enjoying her dessert.

But outside the window – a deep green meadow, sky blue clouds of tree leaves, a cornflower sky, a pink barn – peace.

So Many Girls,

and all of them possessed of something: *Girl with Black Cat, Girl with Tulips, Spanish Girl, Tambourine Girl, Girl with Green Eyes*; but really, for you, right now at least, there is only one girl, and that girl is Kandinsky's painting protégée, Olga.

Yes, she is part of the avant-garde. Part of the *intelligentsia*. A group of Russian, forward-thinking artists and intellectuals. Yes, she is a painter like you. Yes, she is passionate, intense, forthright, loving. Yes, she is in love with you.

But what about this life you've created for yourself? What about this family who lives around your work, surrounds it like the fortifications of an old walled city? What about your wife's practical love, devoted to the protection of your work, your safety?

Do you really want to start again, recreating your life, the way you do periodically in your painting? Do you really want to risk everything with your family, the way you do with your painting? Can you do it? Are you that strong? Is it wise to do something that you are not strong enough to do?

Girl with Green Eyes, 1908

The beautiful sea-foam green behind her left shoulder, to match her eyes. The intense bright vermillion and carmine cape to complement them. And then above but right behind her, some sky blue vases, one curved, one angular, and an apple green wall beyond.

Her funny, cornflower blue hat barely rests on the auburn hair. Her skin is a porcelain reserved for China dolls, a porcelain you never use.

She has a far away, dreamy look, as if she has a secret, or she is in love. Her lips are a shiny, plain red, frank and welcoming.

Girl with Black Cat, 1910

The cat is in her lap, enveloped in her arms, asleep. You can barely see it, on the background of her navy shift. But its paws rest on her knees, languid, so you know this cat is asleep, trusting.

She looks forlorn, ugly almost, with her over-red cheeks, dark almost black cap of hair, severe lines of eyes and brow. Only the sea-foam background wall, and coral base behind her is beautiful. The yellow chair is too bright, and her bone white blouse under the shift is too subdued.

Girl with Tulips, 1910

The auburn hair is almost red, the pose is odd, sitting but looks like standing, hands clasp, in a mock demure stance. The tulips in their vases come up sharp and pointed, like paint brushes, and the larger, cement gray vase, with daubs of carmine looks like a palette.

The red table echoes the daubs, and her hair. Behind, cornflower wall, ochre floor. Her body: bone white blouse, black skirt with silver belt. Everywhere large swaths of color, except for the paint-brushy tulips and the cement gray vase.

58 rue Madame, Paris, 1909

In Paris, at 58 rue Madame, forty of your paintings are housed. It is not a gallery. It is not even a museum. It is the home of Sarah and Michael Stein. In San Francisco, Sarah collected artworks. Then she and her husband moved to Paris, along with Leo and Gertrude.

Now that Gertrude has concocted a fake rivalry between yourself and P., she no longer collects your work. She feeds you scrambled eggs instead of omelets if you try to visit her, as her way of showing her disdain and disrespect for you.

You have the Cone sisters. You have Shchukin. But you know, at any moment, it could all go away, and you'd be left with no source of funding to take care of your family.

Instead of despairing, you try to use this knowledge to force yourself in new directions when you are reluctant to go. You force yourself to be fearless, and soldier on.

La Danse, 1909

Pink, fleshy pink, giant, dancing in a circle, stolen from your own painting *Bonheur de Vivre*, (or re-used, as you will claim later about so many motifs) – five, deep blue above, deep green below. Then a second version for Shchukin, still giant-sized canvas, flesh color turns reddish brown, darker color, darker mood.

Or blue dancers alone, like the blue nude, *Nu Blu*. They are always dancing, always women, (though sometimes men), always outside (though sometimes in a chapel, or on a large arched wall or triptych). They are always gay, always happy, always suspended in the air, feet not touching, never touching the ground, though a toe, suspended may come close enough.

They are very very large, or very very small (though sometimes average, but rarely). They are always rapturous, they always recall spring, (never winter), though sometimes summer. They are always naked, never clothed. They are always skinny, though sometimes curvy, sometimes fleshy. They are always *gamine*. Always *apache*.

Music,

and painting use the same notes, the same shades, nuances, sharp and flat, harmonic and dissonant, melody and refrain, chorus. A Matisse painting uses the same colors as Debussy's score uses notes. Matisse's joy is Debussy's melancholy; Matisse's spring is Debussy's *Spring*.

Color is energy; color is light,

and so must we be light. Everything made of light, appearing solid, moveable, malleable, destructible. Destructive. The brightest colors are tumultuous, vibrating at the highest speeds, pumping out energy like the rolling and crashing of waves, the ripple of a horse's mane as it gallops across the beach at the water line.

Why do we see things as solid? As motionless? Windless, the leaves still sway, moonless, the tides still pull. You pull oxygen into your lungs, suddenly, full of wonder at it all, everything bright, fast, moving. Spinning gyroscope of vermilions, carmines, mauves, violets, cinabrese, ochre and indigo.

Luminous, translucent, phosphorus, quicksilver dawn, light breaking, earth turning, a rush of wings.

Cassis, 1909

Chalk cliffs, fishermen mending their nets, gulls hanging above them, gliding left to right and back again. Twinkling light. An artists' community. Comradery and commiseration.

Painting Classes, Paris, 1909

One can't teach another to paint, can they? You can offer your opinion, as a master practitioner. You can convey what you've learned from experience. You can create an atmosphere of support, comradery, even.

Issy, Fall 1909

Shchukin commissions the large canvas, *Dance and Music*, which pays handsomely. And so to Issy-les-Molineaux, to the big house in a tree-lined suburb, its dappled light, just big enough for the family and the dog, just far enough from Paris there will be a delay of a day or two before you hear the latest news, and then it won't matter anymore. You can take a train into the city, meet your collectors or dealer at the 19 Quai St. Michel studio, if you need to conduct business.

You have a vast studio built, exactly to your specifications, where you can work on large canvases. Family life is centered around quiet times when you work, and raucous times when you allow the family to view your art.

Collioure, 1909

You made friends here, with Maillol, the great sculptor of volumes, with his forceful, imposing shapes, and their soft but strong, beautiful lines. You loved the contrast, the volumes, if not the forcefulness, which you felt predicted, maybe even prophesized the wars to come.

But friends are always solace, someone with whom to share the frustration of work. Collioure: a safe escape, a getaway from the politics of the art world in Paris, the petty rivalries, the dealers and collectors, uproars of shows, bad reviews, the fake ruptures whipped up by the press. You've never liked meanness, but more than that, you've never liked how it comes between you and your work, like a fog descending, so you can't see clearly anymore.

Spain, 1910

Where you find the line. Where you find the spiritual root inside the relaxation and contemplation of enclosed gardens, with their fish ponds, lemon and orange trees, pomegranate and palm. All this will stay to haunt you, to play out endlessly in canvas after canvas.

Where you find pattern and arabesque. Where you find a way to sink the foregrounded objects into the background.

Where you find relief from ridicule, humiliation, failure, poverty, worry. Where you rest and dream. Where you acquire the goal of reducing things to their essence, to the pure expression of truth. The calm in that.

Goldfish

They are always the same fish. They appear and reappear. They are always goldfish. Sometimes they are more red, sometimes more gold, sometimes an orangey red, or orangey gold. They are usually on a table next to the open window that looks out always, to the sea, where little sailboats, masts akimbo, tilt in the wind, (not at windmills), with a backdrop of cirrus clouds. The tablecloth underneath the fishbowl is usually decorated with a flower or leaf design. There are never people with the fish, just the fish. Just the fish, please. Yes. That's right.

Soon – women absorbed in contemplation, but now goldfish, which in Tangiers you will discover means men absorbed, watching the goldfish in bars where women are absent. But you don't portray the men absorbed, only their object of absorption, the goldfish.

Goldfish. Shiny, reflective creatures, suspended in liquid. Their eyes. Green leaves and purple flowers around, like a pond, like a lotus pond. Disc of table, tawny, tan. A coy peek at the arm of one chair, seafoam green, and latticed.

Always a cylindrical bowl, with a mouth as wide as its sides – not a round conventional fishbowl, whose edges curve in to the mouth. La bouche.

In another version the yellow cat is the focus, the fish his desire. In this version you can see the orange window frame and red window, you can see the childlike meadow in blues and greens (out the window), you can see the red with purple flowered walls of the room. Instead of the lotus pond evoking green leaves with purple flowers, there is a multicolored bouquet, and of course, the two lemons, one orange.

Soon, fish will become the ocean, will become seaweed, will become wide swaths of patchwork ocean waves seen from the air above the white seabirds. Soon.

Olga Meerson, Painter, Intellectual, Russian Avant-Garde

Olga's friend, the writer Thomas Mann, said that yearning is power, possession is weakness. Do you agree? It is often said an artist feeds on longing. You create this situation safely, in the studio, with your models, or did before Olga, and will again after her. But Olga is not a model, she is a painting student.

Of course, it's unsettling for you to see such a brilliant painter such as Olga, but with no safety around her, no family. She had Kandinsky as a master, and so many lovers. She is so forthright in her love for you, with her declarations and her letters, but it only terrifies and discomfits you more, because you know that for now you need your family to sustain your work. She is bold, reckless – but not strong.

She lacks the temperament to find what she needs to sustain her, and everything is against her anyway, because she is a woman. You hate to think she will burn brightly for a short time. You want her to endure. When you're young and idealistic you can live on the edge of disaster, but not forever. She is already thirty-three. She needs to pull back a little, gather some protection around her, but everything tells her to throw herself forward with all her intensity and vigor.

She is the only woman who will pose nude for you now, but though you do, you can't bear to pose for her, and even worse, can't bear the reaction to your canvas *Spanish Woman*, (your first triangles), so you pull it from the Salon des Indépendants this spring.

You may love her now; you may soon find that you will always love her, and when she is gone you will allow Lydia to comfort you. You will tell Lydia her story. But she is too dangerous for you now – even, for herself. You need a less intense, calmer, stable love, that does not burn so bright.

The Politics of Use

So, how do you employ models, places, goldfish, cats, lemons and oranges, for your painting, without misusing them? If you afford a living being her dignity, whether it be a model or a goldfish, is that enough? How do you convey that the image on the canvas is a fiction, not a representation? By flattening out the depth? By intensifying color? By elongating the line? By distilling the form to its essence?

Olga lived and died a painter. Lydia planned to be a doctor, but the October Revolution derailed her plans. Amélie was happier, thrived in fact, after she left you and joined the Resistance. Marguerite we cannot speak of; it's too painful.

Is this all your fault? Or does centuries of aggression and abuse come down on women, slamming them like a landslide? You found good jobs for your models, jobs in shops. You taught as many women painters as men. Is it your fault it is so much more difficult for them to go forward? Must you give up your art to fight their cause?

You were never political. Still, you reflect on these things. You worry. The tyranny of your art has both made and ruined your life. You do not want it to ruin anyone else's. But you do not want the tyranny of centuries of man's stupidity to ruin them either. But it has; you must face it, even if you cannot bear to face your own part in it.

The Russians, The English and alas, The Americans

Stop for a moment to think about this: why are none of your collectors European?

It's the Russians in Shchukin, English and Americans in the Steins and Cones who buy your work. Why not the French? Belgians? Swiss? Italians? Spanish?

Shchukin once confessed your paintings ease the pain of his wife's death, his sons' and brother's suicides. For Sarah Stein, it is something else: to her, you are the hope and future of painting. For the Cone sisters, it is affinity, and perhaps a rebellion against Gertrude. Gertrude, who interferes in your life, second hand, with collectors, with friends, now with the press, much more than you would like.

Red Fish, Fish Tank, 1911

Painting, like sculpture, is stationary, but these artists talk only of movement, and depict only movement. These fish are not floating motionless. These women are not dancing motionless, they are not even sitting motionless. They are looking, moving, wondering, watching. The waves are not motionless, the boats, the masts akimbo are not motionless.

Move me.

Even though the ***red fish return***, and the yellow cloth, for six years the palette deepens, portraits of women become Moroccan in turbans, puce and ochre, embroidered caftans, then –

Red Studio, 1911

Red: the first color, the shortest light wave, the clay pot, the drawing on the cave, blood, desire, anger, the way to attract the horns of a bull. Red ochre, iron oxide, hematite.

The red studio series of paintings: simple room, sparsely furnished, your own paintings at odd angles, askew on the walls, a wood stove, a lopsided stool, perhaps a plain wood table or cracked easel, a Parisian, swirl-armed, daffodil-yellow divan – a bright fabric draped unselfconsciously across it. Drenched in red. Percolating in red. Marinated in red. Steeped in red.

The studio where you see yourself as: basic yet avant-garde, lusty yet chaste, entrenched yet aloof, bloody yet exsanguinated. The invisible observer. The anonymous conduit for grace, for art. Not all-knowing, on the contrary, you are blank, a clean channel like the shafts in the pyramids, through which light is reflected and energy is conducted in waves to the canvas.

In the future we will not see red in the chapel at Vence: only the pure earthiness of lemon sun, cerulean blue sky, and the greenest verdigris of leaf. Not the animal earthiness of blood. The stations of the cross, laid out in a crude black pen on white tile, like a sanitarium, like an asylum for believers, to stand before faith and (against their will) have their impurities hosed off, to stand before faith – cured.

With Picasso, 1911

They like to pretend you are not friends, but only competitors. The press and Gertrude make as much trouble as they can about it. The fact is, though you can both learn from each other, he is too young for you to feel any rivalry. He is not competing as a peer; he is trying to outshine a friend he also considers a master. In the other's canvases, you get each other to see approaches and processes you otherwise could not. You aspire to similar goals. But his result is often revolting to you.

So, you visit him when he is sick, and he comes horseback riding with you when he is well. Let the press make their dramas. It is all theater. Your friendship will outlast their gossip.

Twos, Threes

Twos are easy: pairs.

Threes are the number of choice for design, three objects, like three muses, preside over the still life, three-legged stool, three-legged Issy Dog, three-legged easel, three objects on the tabletop, three fish, three decorative balls in a shallow bowl.

Where do they meet? Two-thirds has been claimed as the magic proportion – golden mean, or two stamens three pistils, or families, two parents three children, like your own family of wife, daughter and two sons.

Like many artists, you repeat, you embed secrets, hints, themes (and then disclaim them). In twos and threes they emerge, smiling at the viewer: three cobalt-violet dancers, three lapis-lazuli musicians, three Egyptian-blue guitars, two cinabrese models, three vermillion oranges, two yellow-ochre lemons.

Acanthus, 1911

So deep and rich, like a layer cake, sink into the purple ground, pulled out again by the citrine leaves and moss leaves in the foreground. Drawn to a yellow umbrella shape in the sky, and another orange one, *umbrage*. Honor, respect. Lavender sky smoky, thick, like fog. Mottled edge along the right, like tree bark. The signature stripe of this period.

Main big left side tree has cinnamon bark, with purple undertones, or an illusion? Merges everything purple mauve and lavender in the picture together.

Goats chew their leaves, acanthus.

Morocco, 1912-13

The entire palette changes, shifts. The blues soften and lighten back to Derain's shading and sky, grays enter and persist, a pinkish-mauve appears to complement the gray and blue. Blue-green. Gray seems to be added to everything, no longer bright primary color. The whole composition changes: connected becomes disjointed; solid becomes filled with empty spaces; balanced is knocked off kilter; contentment becomes longing to re-solidify, rebalance, reconnect. Coordinated color schemes becomes chaos of grass greens, burnt oranges, slates, indigos, tawny beiges, all with the gray-infused foundation. Hot Mediterranean becomes cool north Africa, as if seen through a haze. But a haze of what? When was North Africa ever cool?

Letters to Amélie, initial sketch for *The Moroccans* – Morocco, Tangiers – October 1912

In your letters you draw pictures of yourself: forlorn, hapless, discombobulated, comic. You miss her, and you tell her as much, but you want her to forgive you for going away to paint.

Sometimes you sketch out scenes you see: a market, people in conversation, you on a fishing boat, teetering over the side. Sometimes you draw the market, situate yourself amongst the rugs, and brass tea kettles, beehives and burlap sacks of color. You draw the arabesque curve of the enclosure above you.

This time you sketch what will become *The Moroccans*, a group of men sitting in a circle on the floor in the café, the hanging lamps above. It is clear: nothing like the abstraction the finished painting will become.

Palm Leaf, 1912

Ice cream milky orange and blue-green alternate with gray, the palm itself aquamarine tease of stripes for leaves, fanning to the left of green hints, gray and dark gray trunk, cylindrical. Top right green tree leaves, and a swatch of black and gray along the left side like a stripe. Something light citrine bottom left to balance top right greenery. It swims. You could swim in it, except for the orange triangle behind the palm itself, and of course the palm itself. But the large color swathes are swimmable. Color swim. Swim in color. Tahiti beckons. The sea has always been there, Nice. Now it beckons bigger, brighter, glare, silvery glare.

Top left, a hint of gray above the blue-green, almost mimicking the curvature of the earth. Palm tree seen from space? Distorting lens or seeing the real curve?

Standing Moroccan in Green, 1913

This Moroccan man, he doesn't stare at you – the viewer, the painter. He is staring off to his left. Glaring really. The expression is rudely defiant. (Perhaps they do not consider defiance rude in their culture.)

He stands straight. He is aligned. Two swaths of background color divide him: a third of him against a backdrop of cornflower, the other two thirds of him against a backdrop of green. The high collar shirt is a grey with green top, the cornflower side of his turban and beard are green, reflection from the dark green robe, perhaps, that hangs, confidently, relaxed, from his shoulders. A strap seems to hold it, slung over his shoulder, and that leads the eye to a brown and rust border down the middle of the robe. Similar decorations are found on the collar, sleeves. The robe appears to be hooded.

Sienna arms appear from the robe, sienna highlights his face on the (left – his left) green-background side.

He churns animosity: *Outsiders, colonizers*, you imagine him thinking. He hums with a dignity though, underneath all that hostility: a dignity, more subtle than what appears to be animosity. Maybe he sees defiance as strength?

How well do you see him? Do you see inside him? Will he let you in? Can you get in unwittingly, or without his wanting you to?

Is the discomfort in his face your discomfort? Painting a man?

For he is a man. Though different than you. A youngish man. Thirties, maybe even twenties. A slim chance of forties.

When we think in decades, it signals that we are getting old. We didn't think in decades before. We thought of childhood, youth, and now. That is all.

What is this standing Moroccan in a green robe thinking of? How does he see time? Is there only the present? Is there a regrettable past? Is there hope in the future? Or only in paradise?

Paradise is a garden. Moroccan gardens are secret gardens, enclosed by tall, adobe fences. They have abundant date and palm, fig and almond trees, yet these gardeners are living in the desert. They have a desert and the sea. They have a sea and an ocean. They have a Strait of Gibraltar, Spain just above, the Americas much farther to the west. They have so much. The intoxication is almost as perfumed and fabric'd as a Tamil love poem.

All is longing.

Does your belief shape how you engage time? What does he believe? Who are his North African gods? Can he speak of them?

Will his sister model for you? Will he kill you? Will it be safe for her to model for you if he sits off to the side, guarding her, watching her, making her safe? Or is your painter's gaze, in itself, a violation? Will she be wrapped in layers of gauze? Scarves?

Portrait of Mrs. Samuel Dennis Warren, 1913

A ghostly sketch, the long nose, and darkly-etched eyes and brows forming a cross on her oval face. Skinny necked, a little cap of curls, an expression of utter despair, grief down to the bones. Uncanny.

Portrait of Mme Matisse, 1913

She is skinny and spare now, and quite unreal, like all your portraits of this period. Not only does she lack depth, but she lacks essence. Her neck, face and hair are ashen gray, like blank canvas, eyeless, with dark sockets, mouth a black line, nose to eyebrows – one continuous line like a fish grapple. The navy jacket and skirt are elegant, with the teal blouse, and signature orange stripe used almost like a scarf. That orange and the pink rose in the black cap are the only brightness. Behind her teal chair, a navy and indigo background looms up, crowds and flattens her into the surface of the canvas.

This grim style will not make sense until after the Great War, as if you foresaw it. And it will not be collectable until after the second war.

Kees van Dongen's Fancy Dress Ball, March 1913

So, former meat porter turned society scandalizer (and painter) van Dongen throws a costume party like ten years ago, when you were all broke and unexhibited artists; except now, half the guests are socialites, because he paints canvases for them, and because his peekaboo painting was thrown out of the Autumn Salon last fall.

You can tell the artists from the socialites, because the artists have burnt-cork moustaches and their costumes are home-made. The socialites' costumes are stylish and shop made. They do not laugh at themselves as easily or uproariously as the artists. But they do have irony.

There is no shame in meeting new collectors, Amélie says, but how can they take you seriously as a painter when you are dressed as a carnival strong man in a turban?

Armory Show, Chicago, 1913

And so, in America, they blame you for everything that is wrong, apparently, with European art, even though in Europe, you are forgotten entirely, because Cubism is now the rage.

You laugh at the irony, but inside you are sick at heart. You play the violin for comfort.

Despite your eclipse by Cubism, and because of some newspaper articles, André Level sells your 1905 paintings at six times what he paid you for them, while you and your family continue to go hungry.

You miss Paris, so on New Year's Day 1914, you move your now large family back to your student building at 19 Quai St. Michel. It's Marquet's studio, on the floor below your old studio, but just as small and destitute. You keep the Issy house, of course, and return there in the summer to work on your Back series and Jeannette series of sculptures. The American public hates those too.

Your students, like everyone else, are wild over Bergson lectures at the College de France. Everyone is talking about the vital spark, and looking for paintings that have it. Prichard insists yours do. The spark. The Chinese call it *chi*. The Hindus insist it is *breath*. Socrates called it *daimon*. You think it is the distillation of energy that sustains life, and the secret of your work.

Second One-Man Show, Gurlitt Gallery, Berlin, July 1914

Not just a one-man show, but a retrospective. The German gallery sends a representative to convince Sarah and Michael Stein to lend their nineteen paintings for the show.

You are proud but sanguine. The only thing that could stop this now, the only thing that could ruin it, is a war – a war that spreads all across Europe. No, it is not funny. But it is ironic.

Germany declares war on France, August 2, 1914

You can't paint, so you play the violin. In the Tuileries gardens the soldiers report for duty, lining up in squadrons in neat grids.

The residents of Paris are also in lines, but at the bank and the butcher. The buses stop running. People talk about when the coal supply will run out, but most don't think the war will last that long.

Your tiny three-room studio at 19 Quai St. Michel becomes the family home, temporarily, for you, your wife Amélie, daughter Marguerite, and sons Jean and Pierre.

In three weeks, forty thousand French will die in Charleroi, and Germany will take Belgium. Your house in Issy is taken over by the army.

You hate the language of war: Theater of War, requisitioned, artillery battery, penetrated. It is disgusting. Revolting. But not nearly as much as the torture of the soldiers who are asked to live outside in the rain and snow, their feet rotting off, so they can kill each other.

So, you manage to get your family on a train to Collioure. All the Parisians are taking trains south. You remember the seaside town happily, and even get your old house back on the avenue de la Gare. But now a street name with Train Station in it sounds like war to you. Juan Gris and his family are there, staying with Pierre's tutor. Without his German art dealer Kahnweiler, Gris has no monthly stipend, so you try to help.

You are worried about your mother, in the north, but in trying to get to her, you are stopped in Bordeaux, where you find out this war will last much longer than through the fall. You go on to Paris, where you try to take care of some business. There you persuade Gertrude to help Gris through the war. She doesn't. You never speak to her again. War is a time of endings.

You try and fail to get money from your own art dealer at Bernheim-Jeune, even from Shchukin, but since November, no monies can leave Moscow for Paris. So, you have another retrospective show at the Montross Gallery in Manhattan.

The war is only four months old, yet three million soldiers have died.

Woman on High Stool, 1914

A skinny woman in a charcoal room, wearing a charcoal shirt, and blue-green skirt. She sits on a skinny high stool, in front of an orange drafting table. The room is so gray that we are desperate for the blue-green and orange, as desperate as the woman looks desolate, her barely etched face, under a forlorn cap of hair.

It will be the last canvas that Shchukin acquires before he loses everything. When you see him in Paris, he is full of zest, just in from a Portofino swimming-and-sunbathing, coffee-under-striped-umbrellas vacation. Why he chooses such a yearning canvas is a mystery; but he will never be happy again.

Interior with a Goldfish Bowl, 1914

It's as if your vision has narrowed to a space of five square meters: the iron scrollwork on the window guard, the table in front of the window. The palette is blacks, greys and bone white, which makes us desperate for the deep vermillion orange and satisfyingly carmine fish. A black stripe runs through the middle and supports the fishbowl and range on its table, with gray stripes on either side, hiding whatever is beyond the window.

You can't see past the window, past this table, past this corner of the room. There is only a fish in a bowl. Only an orange. Only a black scrolled window guard. That is all.

Monet at least had a garden; Cezanne, a mountain, a cathedral.

New Work: 1916-1917

And so begins the new work, the difficult work, spare and skinny, stark, and ugly. The only ugly paintings you'll ever do.

You want to strip to essentials. Find an essence. So, you do a *Bathers* in homage to Cezanne's (after all, your Amélie pawned the emerald from her dowry to buy it), later, in a year, you do your collector and godfather Pellerin's portrait.

Bathers by a River, 1916

They are gray and faceless, with ashen shadows. Their heads are ovals and breasts are perfect circles. The green background has black curved lines in it, suggesting river reeds.

They could be wooden African sculptures. They look essential enough. Distilled. You have your signature stripes, in this case wide vertical bands of gray-blue, charcoal, bone white, black and apple green.

You have changed your work forever, and yet, no one will buy this painting, until a year before you die.

Apollinaire's Party, December 31, 1916

You're turning forty-seven, but the party is for Apollinaire's return from the war, and the launch of his book, *Le Poete Assassiné*. So what if you are a generation older than them: Picasso, Braque, Leger, Gris, Jacob, Cendrars, Modigliani – both Amélie and Marguerite say that it should not matter. But you feel it, like ash in your mouth; when they dance on tables, shoot guns, throw bread, you sit quietly, trying to save whoever is in the line of fire.

The Piano Lesson, 1916

Pierre confesses later that the model for the little boy is indeed himself. He is engulfed by the giant piano. He looks so vulnerable. Everything is so stark, as it should be, for Pierre's music lessons were elaborate (piano all morning, violin all afternoon), strict and grueling.

The canvas is filled with wedges: to the left of the canvas, a green wedge pushes the viewer's eye into the middle of the room. A slate wedge of a metronome sits on the puce table beyond the piano. Above the piano music you can only see the poor little boy's head, so poignant, his right eye wedged out, again in slate. Another gray wedge hides on the left side of the puce piano cover, and a deep black one shadows it.

There are also signature stripes: a chalky blue for the window and coral for the inside wall. In the bottom left of the canvas, a sienna figure reclines, like a tiny bronze sculpture. the black iron scrollwork on the balcony matches that on the piano's music stand.

Quite far away, behind him, a ghost of a woman stands, watching.

The Margarine King: *Portrait of Auguste Pellerin II*, 1917

You wince when people call him the Margarine King. He is your godfather and your first collector. You bring Halvorsen to his home at Neuilly to study his Cézannes.

In his portrait he is skinny, all black, blue-grays and slate, a solemn expression. He's commissioned the portrait. He could be a political cartoon, about the war, its horror and futility. He is all in blacks and browns. His eyes are black, hollow. He sits demurely, his elbows resting on the table, hands clasped, dressed in a black suit and tie, with a bright red pin on his jacket. (We will see this red spot again in the Icarus cut out.) He is staring straight forward.

A whitish object in the painting behind his head matches his beard and his whitish chair. A brown shape seems to come out of the painting and cradle the side of his head. The curve of the brown shape matches the curve of the chair, and that of his arms and bald pate.

Portraits Become Odalisques

become body landscapes as he surrenders to the luxury of a woman's form, the rapture of the body, of the silky curve, subtle muscles, smelling of peach, of soap and salt. Of comfort.

1917, and so to Nice, slowly,

to make a home, to stay there, until forever comes. To know you are there. To know when you travel, this is where you will come back. To focus. To find the essential nature of the thing. Not to find the essential, not to find the essential in nature, but to find the essential nature of the thing. Just one thing. One at a time.

The war is tiresome, horrific, exhausting. The worry. Your parents. You buy a car. Pierre drives you into the hills above Nice. You paint the view out the window: trees, roadway, bushes at the side of the road, meadows beyond, and further, further on, the sea.

Renault Motor Car, Summer 1917

You had no idea what that feeling of freedom would be like, having your own broken down Renault motor car, your son Pierre driving it through the winding roads of Mount Boron, where you could smell the pines and feel the olive trees sweep past you – all so quickly, like a life, or a mad love affair.

Not like the war, the Great War they called it, giving it a depraved majesty, the ugliest violence Europe had seen since the Holy Wars, (Holy War – another glorifying name).

So, you sat, almost complacent in the tight-fitting passenger seat, while Pierre drove you through the hills. Higher and higher. The giant Belle Epoch villas, stacked on the cliffs, whizzed by; the Bay of Angels glittered quick and fast, just below, its sailboats rocking in the choppy water; the lighthouse and jetty revealed themselves in glimpses through the bright orange trumpet flowers.

He is only seventeen, your Pierre. What will happen now, you wonder, with cars, and airplanes, and wars and young people driving and dying.

PART TWO: PERFECT THE LINE

Lorette, 1917

So, you abandon minimalism, reducing to essentials, and paint Lorette every week for a year. What a joy she gives you. Her dark eyes. Her sleek body. The way she looks at you.

Now, they say you learn the fastest, and the most if you love deeply what you are learning. This is the secret of your relationship to your models. You love them with a passion, an ardor, unrestrained. Unconfined. And you submit to it, letting it lead you into a new direction for your painting. Who else does that? Who else paints like you, now?

You find your own way. Suddenly, your paintings no longer look like Fauve paintings or Cubist paintings, they look like Matisse paintings. And they will for the rest of your life. Welcome to now. Welcome to the present. Welcome to your real life, your real paintings. You belong to no school. You are yourself. Your secret is so simple no one sees it: you love each woman along your path.

But with Lorette, (unlike with Olga before her), you are wiser, and she is calmer. You don't show your ardor. You don't let it control you, knock you off balance. You keep it contained, inside yourself, directed toward your work, and toward Lorette herself. The intensity only increases, and you only learn better and faster for it. Oh, joy.

Lorette in Turban and Yellow Jacket, 1917

It is not just the jacket that is yellow. The face and skin bear patches of yellow with peach. Hints of light on turban are a pale yellow. The right top corner of the chair behind is a golden yellow. The left patch of wall beyond is a golden yellow, mixed with ochre and gray.

She stares at you. Intense. Scolding? An admonishment? Reproach? Love, perhaps? A warning? Whimsy? Danger?

Her eyes are so warm, so brown, like chestnuts. Darker than her jacket buttons. But they are not close to the even darker brown, almost black of her hair, eyebrows.

Aside from brown, the only things that are not yellow, black lines or white swaths, are the dark red blotch of her tiny mouth, and the more apple red patch of her chair above her right shoulder.

You will never give her up. Even if you have to. Even if your wife sickens, near death, even if you must leave your family and the safe confines of the Issy house forever.

This war is bringing an end to many things. Your old work, for example, which you assume is destroyed. You cannot imagine a future where, in Moscow, Shchukin lives in a tiny, dark servant's room in his own attic, and gives tours of his own magnificent art collection. Where postwar, as a Russian exile in Nice, Shchukin pretends not to see you on the street, he does not acknowledge your artistic collaboration.

The Music Lesson, 1917

The deep green of trees seems to come into the room behind the piano, where a small boy sits with his mother. Another boy sits on the floor, reading. A violin lays on the puce cover of the piano. A third boy sits outside, gazing at his knees.

The boy at the piano seems focused, the boy on the floor engrossed, their mother happy. But the boy sitting outside seems sad, ostracized, melancholy. Who is that boy? Who is set apart from the family scene?

The final figure is in a painting behind the piano, background as green as the view beyond the window, a figure seated on a high black chair, in a charcoal shirt and blue pants.

Visit to Renoir, December 1917 – Spring 1919, Les Collettes, Cagnes sur Mer

If only you were not so stiff and self conscious, meeting the great master. He will think you odd, but not in the acceptable and welcome way that artists are odd. He will think you oddly formal.

It's your birthday, so self consciousness might be warranted. You want to do something for the great man. Above all, you want to come back to visit, form a friendship, talk about art.

As his children lead you from the studio, through the garden and into the house, it strikes you that you could find this new model that he needs. And so, you do – a seventeen-year-old refugee from Alsace, who looks exactly like the other pink-cheeked, over-stuffed young girls in Renoir's paintings.

The great master is grateful. He can paint again. He credits you. But when, a year into your alliance, in his appreciation, he proposes an exchange of canvases, you are mortified. You feel unworthy. How could this great master think you a peer? A colleague? You are there to learn. You would never consider yourself an equal, the way the arrogant, fifteen-years-younger Picasso considers himself yours.

After the war, you will bring your family to meet his. When Shchukin is in Nice, you will take him as well. But you remain the supplicant, the pilgrim, the worshiper, bringing people as your alms, as your frankincense and myrrh.

Bay of Angels, Nice, 1918

Bright colors at last return: purple, bright new-leaf green, odalisques returned to France become nudes again, sitters become women and models, flowers bright pink, vases a sparkly silver.

The Armistice Signed, 11 November 1918, Nineteen Quai St. Michel Studio, Paris

The crowd in the streets dances in unison. You were too young in the last war to remember this, and anyway – you were not in Paris. You try not to lift your head up from the canvas or Lorette at 19 Quai St. Michel, where you work nonstop at canvas after canvas. The elation in the streets seeps through the windows and infuses the studio. It kicks up the dust, which glints in the sun streaks as it passes through the rays. Lorette shifts on the divan, but never takes her eyes off you. She smiles a little at what she hears, what she imagines of the crowd in the street. The men are walking on short stone walls along the Seine. The women are laughing. The men are noticing how the women throw back their hair when they laugh. The mood of abandon sweeps them along, an upsurge of relief and hope, blotting out four years of panic and deprivation.

Lorette tilts her head back, imagines it, runs her fingers through her hair. Euphoria. It was there before the war, in the electric energy of this city, Paris, and in the new cars and planes. But no one can predict or imagine the postwar euphoria that will bring Coco Chanel's cropped haircuts, dangly bead necklaces, stretchy jersey fabric and loose hanging dresses for women, freeing them from the corset, the skirt rail, and from pinned-up long hair, all at one blow. They will not predict the sudden rise in wealth and wild behavior, the recklessness, the lawlessness, the jazz.

You already feel this electricity running through you and Lorette. You'll paint it in the Odalisques and the bouffy harem pants, and the mixed prints on the walls, the screens, the draped divans, the tablecloths. You will plumb its heart.

Violinist at the Window, 1918

Is this how you see yourself? A blank shape at the window, hoping for some wisdom to come through from the sky. You play the violin for that sky, cradled between shoulder and chin.

The sky is such a deep carmine red, with clouds underneath. It's as if you're playing to the storm, a tempest, hurricane, perhaps. Your jacket and pants burn ochre, and the checked floor below is not nearly as red as the sky.

Your head is bulbous and white like the clouds beyond. Are you the messenger? Is your music stretching to reach the gods?

Storm, Bay of Angels, Nice, January 2, 1919

The calm bay turns violent. Wind rips through palm trees. Waves surge against the breakwater. The sky turns to slates and purples. The shutters of your room's window rattle and fall away. Windows and then mirrors break.

You choose a canvas and, sitting, you secure it between knees and elbows. You have paper too. You draw and paint whatever you can. For the first time, the intensity of a place matches your own intensity. Its violence matches your violence.

After the storm, you sit, surrounded by line drawings and the wet canvas. You stand at the window, safe now, and look outside at the gauzy illumination, the storm's luminous wetness reflecting on the torn palm trees and battered hotels, on the sidewalks and grassy lawns, on the sand and sea. It's not an illumination you've seen before.

Old Town, Nice is a Theater, 1919

You love to walk the streets. They are so unlike you, these Niçois. They scream at each other, and then embrace each other. They gesticulate, hands in the air. They throw fish and cabbages at each other. They throw mops from second floor windows, which hit the street at odd angles and ricochet into passersby.

You want to laugh. You feel you are in an opera. A comic opera. Who are these people, to make them so dramatic? Not really Italian – they have a different style of theatricality than the Italians, but not really French. Not the French reserve. Some hybrid, you think.

As with your painting, you love to be the watcher, the one who is not in the frame, in the drama. You can molt, become someone else, with no one looking.

Costumes and Props: The Purple-Striped Robe

The purple-striped full-length robe, the wardrobe, the props. The robe on a reclining woman, her feet hidden, tucked under her, in green harem pants and green floral blouse, leaning on a green pillow, on an oddly grey pinstripe suit covered divan. A darker green pinstripe background, and the mustard signature stripe on the left side. A burgundy floor.

Another: a seated woman in the purple robe, resting her high head against her knuckles, black beads of a necklace, floral gray blouse, with lighter, floral green skirt, barefoot. Beside her, and slightly foregrounded, oranges and lemons surround the gray vase, sprouting a riot of red and lavender, and white dahlias, set on a scrolled gray table, this time the divan is bright orange, the wall behind mustard with orange stripes, the window gray with white stripes, the floor black, checkerboard etched.

A Third: seated woman, arms spread out along the green and mustard divan, in white neck beads, a white and gray floral blouse, the same moss green pants, the same vase, but red and white, the flowers all yellow, the oranges apples, the lemon still lemon, the table still gray arabesques. But the left wall is dark green with black squirrels, and the right wall is black with red and white flower designs, like a swatch of fabric hung on the wall, the floor below a pale grey rug, with slate-grey stitching, the floor below the black with etched checkers. And shoes now! The first black slippers on demurely crossed feet.

Renoir, Les Collettes, Cagnes dur Mer, Spring 1919

You don't want to see the Master when he is dying. You don't want to face any death after the horrible war, but especially not his death, even if it is a death from old age, not from brutality, torture, killing.

In the big bed, he seems frail, despite his bulk. He thanks you, for finding him a new model, for getting him painting again after so many months. There is so much to be thankful for, it seems, when you are dying. There is so much to remember.

He seems at peace in a way you struggle to understand. How can one be at peace with giving up this life? With giving up the struggle and the fight to find what you are trying to achieve in painting? Yes, he is acknowledged as the master painter of his time in France, but what does that matter, you think. What matters is to fight on, to struggle, to keep looking for what you are looking for in the act of painting. Nothing else matters. And you can't do that if you are dead.

But the body fails, eventually. He has accepted it, his family has accepted it, and so, you must as well. You say your goodbyes, but something in you rebels at this, sees it as some renunciation, as some unnecessary and unwanted closure.

Snubbed in Nice, 1919

What do you do when Shchukin passes you on the street and looks the other way, just keeps walking? Are you supposed to run after him? Apologize? For what? To be obsequious is not in your nature. To prostrate yourself is not in your nature. Your whole being rebels at the idea. You cannot force the gesture.

Plus, you are simply stunned. It was so unexpected. He always visits you when he is on holiday in Italy and comes to Nice. Now he is acting like he doesn't know you.

Is this political? Does he blame you for losing his art collection to the October Revolution? For being made a servant in his own mansion? The tour guide to what was once his own collection? Is it personal? He always depended on your canvases for solace. Now they've been taken from him, and he has no solace.

You think this is not your fault. You think you should not be blamed. You think there is some misunderstanding, and that perhaps when Shchukin cools off perhaps it can be cleared up.

Who Will Buy the New Work? 1919

The Steins have sold the early work to a Dane, Tetzen-Lund is his name, and that man plans to keep it in his apartment in Copenhagen. Prichard can't climb out of the nightmare of being a prisoner in the war, (and who can blame him?), and Purmann is trapped in postwar Germany.

So, no buyers. What happens now? You and Halvorsen tried to convince the Steins not to sell, but Michael simply denied it, while Sarah cast furtive glances at the emptied spaces on the wall where your paintings had been.

So, none of what the critics call the early work is in France. None is on view. It's gone forever, except in photographs and newspaper clippings of old shows.

Panic, 1919

You see now, that this will happen over and over: what you've been working on for months or even years will be finished, and it will be time to pursue a new line of inquiry. How will you do this? It won't be hard to abandon what you are doing, for the simple reason you'll be finished with it. And it won't be hard to find the new line of inquiry, because it will have been pestering you for months. But there will still be that opening salvo, that panic, of starting something new, something you are not yet immersed in. You'll hear the voices of family and critics saying don't do it, keep on at the other line. But you must satisfy your curiosity. You must pursue line, color, balance, composition, in whatever form that inquiry takes you, for the whole of your life, mustn't you?

So, you leave behind what they will come to call the early work of 1916-1917. You do not know what is coming. I know it is models, interiors, odalisques, harem pants and patterned screens and wallpaper. The critics will groan. But you will press on.

Woman with Green Parasol on Balcony, 1919

Antoinette Arnoud is sublime, the perfect French type now: ashen, alarmingly thin, so stylish and chic. You love her, and you could draw and paint her indefinitely. You need no other.

For the shutters you choose a perfect cornflower, the sea beyond is violet. The parasol is emerald green, and her so, so sophisticated stockings are aubergine, or a deep eggplant color.

The rest is so stone it is almost blank canvas: the balustrade, her blank face and dress, the balcony floor. You do add a vertical signature stripe in lemon on the right side, and a red carpet stripe just inside the shutters. Then of course, a hint of brown for the seat of the chair, and black outlines of chair, dress, balustrade, legs, shutter panels.

Of course, Breton thinks it is something – important, he says, the most important since *Goldfish with Palette*, and everyone listens to Breton now, so that is satisfactory.

You will paint her again like this, the shutter becoming door, the stockings lightening to violet, daubs of color on the shift dress, the head with its face, the umbrella a lighter, translucent emerald. No lemon stripe, but more red carpet inside the door.

The next time she'll be in a floral dress, the palm trees will show through the window, the sea will be windy and little waves will be starting up in the bay. She'll be facing the water this time, instead of you, and the balustrade will have violent tints to it.

In yet another version, the umbrella will be puce, Antoinette facing you flat and staring, her hand by her beautiful face. Now the balustrade is slate grey, the sky bright blue, the palm tree is laughing, because you can't really see the bay. The dress has ochre and black splotches, almost like a watercolor.

Antoinette is a dream. You are dreaming, here on the bay of Nice. With its beautiful colors, and glinty reflections. How can you ever go back now?

Bloomsbury at the Leicester Galleries Show, 1919

You want to know: who are these crazy young people, so concerned with style and fashion? How does being in the group augment them? They are skinny, which always makes you suspicious. One of the young men smokes a pipe, one of the young women twirls and hangs on her taller sister.

They call them Bloomsbury, after a section of London, painters and writers, in couples of all sorts. To you they are just crazy; they have bought up every new canvas you had at the Leicester Galleries show in London. All in a swoop, like a falcon seizing a mouse. You do not like to be the mouse.

Issy Dog: *Tea in the Garden*, 1919

We never talk about the things we give up: family life, comfort, love, a community you created. Or simply having people around, absorbed in their own lives, lives running parallel to your own.

Such an uncharacteristic nostalgia, the lovely filtered light, canopy of trees. Staring women, seated in high back chairs at a small round pedestal table. All in seven or more different shades of green, the green of nostalgia. Envy perhaps, of not being satisfied with such a life. Not feeling in the bones it is enough.

But here below, you have painted yourself, in the dog. The forlorn, self-mocking expression you use in self-portraits, in the scribbled drawings in margins of letters home. The hapless, off kilter, broken nosed expression of regret and sorrow, trying to be humorous. The head low, shoulders hunched, as if the dog expects to be scolded, or even struck. But the staring women seated at the drinks-laden table see only the anonymous viewer, the painter, standing aloof.

People will look back on *Tea in the Garden* as your last work at Issy, and say it is sad, nostalgic, but is it? It seems winkingly humorous, the dog is you, scruffy, discombobulated, forlorn.

Sad, forlorn, relinquishing: Issy Dog.

You do not know that "Post War" will become "Between the Wars," that the Issy Dog will become the Aix en Provence *Boss Dog*, will later appear in *New Yorker* drawings, and elsewhere, as will many other forlorn, self-mocking, beleaguered stand-ins for their artist/owners.

Marguerite, January 1920

Being unable to breathe triggers terror; there is no way to subdue that reaction. So, when Marguerite's throat won't heal after her larynx reconstruction, you know she is in an almost constant state of panic. Perhaps that's why her body pushes out the metal or rubber they try to use to keep her breathing vent open.

How odd that twenty-five years from now, the only thing that will ever free her from the constant pain and terror of her own body suffocating her, is to barely survive being held prisoner and tortured by the Nazis. Her body is so long-suffering, so tough by then, that she can endure any pain another inflicts – because what her body has inflicted on itself over so many years is so much worse.

Strangely, paradoxically, this experience of imprisonment and torture frees her, makes her euphoric, otherworldly – as if she has cheated death, as if she finally has realized that she is not the weak, frightened person she thought she was, but rather a brave, strong woman fighting for her country and her child.

But that is (twenty–five) years in the future.

The Nightingale, 1920

Now the panic comes, the way it did when you arrived in Morocco. There, it could be that sickness from glare or heat, but in Paris, it's plain you've no idea where to begin. You hate this disease, this paralysis, and wish you could rid yourself of it, but don't know how. Sometimes you want to give in to it, and just live in a few square blocks around your studio, paint. But your curiosity and others demands draw you out; the need to make a living, accept commissions, and meet collectors forces you to accept others' challenges instead of your own, which are less frightening, because they don't have deadlines, they are not subject to others' rages and scrutiny, to a performance at the end of it.

But for now, the panic is here. The answer: research. Preparation.

***

You notice this young man is slightly amused, ironic as he shows you around the museum. Later you'll learn he is a famous expert on Chinese religion and culture. To you he is just a young man escorting you through a wing of the British Museum for your *Nightingale* costumes research. When in a panic about what to do, how to start, it is always helpful to research.

He takes you through: walls of vases encased in glass, scrolled sculptures in clay and porcelain of men in unbalanced postures and beautiful robes, dogs and lions, emperors and gods, all strategically lit for maximum drama. It is enough to make a start.

***

Theater is a window. Certainly you can look at it like that. Sets are cutouts. Curtain with three masks, costumes with cutouts, mourner robes reappear thirty years later in Vence as priests' robes.

Every costume a priest's robe. Bold triangle, chevron. Natural, baggy linen shorts and ballooning tunic.

The beautiful nightingale replaced by a mechanical clacking bird. Of course, it was a disaster. Everything mechanical is a disaster.

But Diaghilev succeeds and fails with such flare, such drama. Astound me, he says to his minions. It is a voyeur's view onto other artists' collaboration. Your collaboration is more intimate. Two or three at most. The others are not artists necessarily, but models. If they are artists, they are away from their art, earning a living, posing for you.

But Diaghilev puts three or four giant egos in the same practice room. Composer, choreographer, major dancer, and himself.

You are taken out of yourself at these moments. Your bemused view of life and the people in it, rises to the surface of your thought. You look out the window. You listen to the disembodied voices. You hear the ting of piano notes. More voices. You hear the thump of feel on the floor. You turn and see the dancers try a jump or twirl.

When you insist that Diaghilev use a highest quality red worsted for some of the robes, he balks. You tell him the red robes must sing. He doesn't understand: the whole performance must sing, like the lost living nightingale.

He answers with something like, *The red will dance, why must it also sing*?

You are not drawn to dancers as Degas or Rodin are, but you like this clash of giant forces, trying to make art together. You like their respect for the audience: not trying to please the audience, but instead trying to wake them to suddenly seeing the world new.

You like making three dimensional objects that are not sculpture: the robes, the screens, the drop curtains. Later you will come back to this with the cut outs and the priests' robes, and the chapel chairs, podium and candelabras.

You can't help thinking about what the nightingale represents: the emperor dies because he won't accept any other song but the nightingale's. Is this you? Do you refuse to compromise in your work, and refuse to compromise anything for your work?

Is this why the ballet fails? Publicly, Diaghilev blames the choreography, but secretly, your costumes and sets? Marguerite says it is simply too noble, when people want entertainment instead. But you can't help but wonder, is failure written into the story? Is it doomed? Is this why you despaired to start it at all?

Diaghilev rages at failure. He insists, always, that failure is not his fault, but that of others. His art is collaborative, so he can do this so easily. You, on the other hand, rage at studio assistants, distractions, demands on your time. You will not go to Bohain and dismantle your dead mother's house. You will not go to Paris and comfort your grieving wife Amélie when her father dies. When the criticism ramps up too high, you will leave Paris and retreat to Nice and the Hotel Méditerranée to work, saying you can't get anything done in Paris.

You want focus, not distraction. You want to strive for the pure, pine like the Emperor for his nightingale, and die of unhappiness, of frustration, of desire for a perfection you can't achieve.

Seven Canvases in Nice, February-April 1920

So, you leave Marguerite and Amélie at the Quai St. Michel apartment and studio in Paris, and you go back to Nice, to the hotel Méditerranée, to prove you work much better there without the distractions of death, family, the Issy dog.

You pose your model, Arnoud, lounging near the window, the tissue-paper thin, fluttery anemones in pink and lavender, vased on the table, with some oranges and lemons, and you paint, paint, paint.

Parents get old and die, don't they? Love fades. Frustrations mount. You paint. You shut all this out and paint seven canvases until you are satisfied. Now it is April.

When the new paintings are done, you ship them to your family for critique. What your family, the critics, your friends are calling a different direction, looks like the same work to you. In your own paintings, you see the search for line, for color, for balance. Despite the travel, the moves from Paris to Nice and back, the different models, studios at Issy, on Quai St. Michel, and at One Place Charles Felix, collectors, critics, even the different approaches to painting, your intent remains the same. You wonder: how can that be? Why does it remain a secret? Because no one sees it but you.

Pilgrimage: Renoir's Studio 1920-26

For six years, since the great master has died, Renoir's family lets you go back into his studio in the back garden, with its low hanging trees and butterflies. You are grateful they allow this privilege; they seem to enjoy your confirming presence there. Sometimes they bring tea, and you talk.

But in the afternoons, once they leave you alone, as they often do, you study his canvases, his finished and unfinished paintings, to learn what you need for your own.

It seems simple once you discover it, but up until then it remains a mystery: there is no background in his paintings. They are flat. We have returned to the Egyptians, to flatness, to style, not realism. That long struggle the Renaissance painters made to gain perspective in painting, must be abandoned again for your canvases.

One Place Charles Felix, Old Town, Nice

It is so laborious moving into this studio in Nice, you are determined to remain in this studio forever.

The streets are cobbled and narrow. The Niçois live here noisily, yet will shout up at you when you play your violin. Being a northerner, you can't help but admire the violence of their enthusiasms, their rustic living, without hot water or electric lights.

You walk the neighborhood counterclockwise: up and slightly east to the castle, then west to the courthouse and senate houses, further to the Cathédrale St. Réparate, and down the Café Pomel for a coffee. Coming back, down and east again toward the studio, on the Cours Saleya, you rumble into the flower market, buy your tulips and anemones for your still lifes. Your momentum carries you a few more steps east, to the green grocer for bread and oranges. You stop and gaze at the glinty bay before you walk back to your studio again.

The Love for Three Oranges, 1921

What if you loved three oranges? Is that so strange? Would you write an opera about it? Have you ever loved an orange? A walnut, perhaps?

No one would look twice if you said you loved an orange tree, or even better, a date or a fig tree, where you lay underneath its shade, as a child, on hot summer mornings, and listened to your mother, plaintively calling for you. No one looks or thinks twice about nostalgia, childhood memories. But a love for three oranges? Those fruits, plucked from their origin, the tree, those disenfranchised, detached, deracinated things, how do you love three fruits? So frail. So perishable. So removed from their source of life.

You did not love three oranges: you loved two lemons. Your one orange was there only to make a grouping of three. You hid your love well. No one questioned it. Maybe they noticed the theme, but it was lodged among many themes: bright, patterned fabrics; guitars, pianos, music lessons, girls in harem pants, windows, cats, goldfish. Would the viewer say you loved a window, or loved the view? This theme of three lemons repeats in your studio, still life or figure paintings.

But mercifully, Diaghilev did not want you to paint the three oranges of the opera's title. He wanted a drawing of Prokofiev for the opera's program. You do not employ the characteristic irony, humor or self-effacement you use for your own self-portraits. You draw Prokofiev serious, prim, almost dignified, narrow but fleshy, lit up from inside, with thick, pursed lips and an imperious expression. He looks alien: not of this world, not of this country? You put your love of three lemons aside, for Diaghilev, as you would put many other things aside for Diaghilev. In exchange: a costume from *Shéhérezade* for your models to wear when posing, for the odalisques still lives.

Odalisques – Nice, 1921

Arabesque is curved line; curve of the line is movement. Odalisque is a conceit, a nod to the past – Delacroix, Ingres – (Renoir and Manet are too close to nod toward), a little camp, maybe. The costumes – harem pants, Russian blouses, striped robes, chevron robes, are from Diaghilev's ballet collections, past and soon to be past, because you will keep collecting. The backdrops are your own, your collection from here and there. Your roots in a northern France textile-making town, mosaic patterns from Morocco, later, tapa – bark cloth intricate patterns of dark and light, squiggles and turtles, from Oceania, Tahiti; but for now, the rest picked up in markets everywhere, a block away from rue Charles Felix in old town, Nice.

Movement is all. Pattern is repetition, which is restful. But they misunderstand. Not rest as sloth, not rest as pleasure, but rest and repose as relief from overwork. Paradise, not as self-indulgence, but in the spiritual ecstasy of pure beauty. Pure life, like pure form, pure line, pure color. Everything in balance. Everything harmonized. Secret Garden. Paradise. Paradise of line, color, pattern, movement. Glorious.

You know. Why does no one know? Is it really that difficult to understand? Why do they think the worst is true? The stupidest is true? The most obvious is true? Isn't life subtle? Supple? Complex? Complexity to be simplified, made pure. Why not that? Why not pure intentions?

To be continually misunderstood. To be underestimated. To be sullied with the squalor of base intentions.

And yet: work, always work. The only balm. The only consolation against the stupidity and incomprehension of the world. Work, solitude, more work, always the light; and perhaps, carefully, a little companionship.

But, why do critics jump to disparaging conclusions, the minute they see an odalisque? A woman in harem pants? This is what you want to know. They claimed you appropriated and modernized the pastoral with *Bonheur*, did the same for the interior setting in *Harmony in Red*, and for the nude in your very first *Blue Nude* – even the portrait they praise you for modernizing. So why, when they see an odalisque, do they not claim you have appropriated and modernized that? Why do they squawk, balk, bolt, cave, whine that you've gone retro and conservative on them? Have they really looked at these Odalisques?

Rodin sculpted his *Age of Bronze* man with his arm over his head, and a look of being lost in erotic rapture, after the Michelangelo sculptures of the same pose, who look equally rapturous.

A woman in this arm-over-head pose – critics call this: Dream of Desire, after ancient images of Ariadne. But, who is the dreamer?

Whose dream is it? The artist's? The viewer's? The man or woman, him or herself, shown in this pose? And is the dream, a dream of desire? Do we want to desire? Do we envy their erotic rapture? Do we desire their dream? Or are we having the dream? Are they the dream? So, it's not real desire, but a hope or dream of having it?

What if it's not erotic rapture? What if the person in the painting or sculpture simply feels languor? Is it then, a dream of languor?

Ariadne, do not clip your thread; pull us out of this labyrinth.

But you'd rather work than worry. You've temporarily abandoned distilling the essence, to work in volumes. You've borrowed a dancer, an actress, Henriette, from the Pathé studio to model for you. She can twist into athletic, dancer positions. When Marguerite visits, the two girls can play music and chess while you draw and paint them.

Marguerite says not to worry; people want some kindness after the Great War, and your paintings are kind, soothing. Sometimes you wonder if all your work is just a balm to your anxiety. You hope it is to others as well.

The Moorish Screen, 1921

Henriette and Marguerite are in front of the screen with a blue/green floral pattern, and a scalloped top edge. The wallpaper is a sea-green and gold, in a fleur de lys pattern, and the rug, cinabrese, and carmine, in leaf patterns. Three patterns, and the pink and white anemones make a fourth. Their dresses a pale pink, their arms relaxed, legs ending in white pumps. Marguerite stands holding a mirror; Henriette has put down their book onto the round brown table and looks at her. There is amitié between them, a secret pleasure of confidences, in their faces, a budding friendship.

Soon you will take Marguerite dancing. You will take her to see all your artist friends and families along the coast: the Bussys in Roquebrun, the Signacs, Renoir's children at Les Collettes. You will take her shopping to pick out dresses for the models.

The Opera, Monte Carlo, 1922

Marguerite declares you are working Henriette too hard, washing brushes, running errands, here and there, in and out. She has no time to rest, see her boyfriend, go shopping with Marguerite and Amélie. Marguerite says you must take them on a drive. Marguerite says you must take them to the Opera in Monte Carlo.

You take them all: *Matisse and the Women*. Threes are convivial numbers for you, they portend balance, success – you like them. Henriette delights in the lights and fountains and the fancily dressed (fancifully, you think) young flappers from Manhattan in their long shifts and dangly strings of pearls. Henriette thinks Charles Hackett is handsome as Des Grieux, in *le portrait du Manon*, and this makes Marguerite laugh, which for you, makes the entire excursion worthwhile. At the end, Henriette cries, when Jean's love for Aurore triumphs, and the Chevalier Des Grieux allows them him marry the lower class Aurore, where before he forbade it.

For yourself, you look at the colors, vermillion, carmine and cinabrese; the lighting and the way it changes the shades of the colors. You search the lines of the costumes for perfect lines. The emotions of love they portray do not move you. The costumes make you think of Diaghilev, whose season here at the Monte Carlo Opera starts soon; the voices make you think of your doves.

On the drive home, your three women – wife, daughter, model – are damp-eyed, heartsick, and hopeful, for each have gained and lost love; they comfort each other.

Goldfish, Turtle and Issy Dog

Do you laugh at what the critics say? Despair? Ignore them? They say you are the goldfish in your goldfish canvases, the turtle in your *Bathers with a Turtle*, and your dog, in *Tea in the Garden* (even I say that, Issy Dog). But if you are all of those, why are you not the window? Why are you not the lemons and oranges? Why are you not the women? The boys?

Cosmic Space, The Fourth Dimension

When is space cosmic? How do you show it in your canvases? When you flatten the picture plane, so there is no depth, no foreground and background, is that cosmic space? When you have a window, with sectioned shutters on either side, and a transom window above, and other paintings and mirrors on the walls beyond, so there are thirteen different frames (the window being the first), is that cosmic space?

When you strive to perfect line and color, is that spiritual? Do you think about color in space? The colors made when planets are lit by stars? By gasses? The color of an exploding star?

Age Fifty-Four and All Your Collectors Are Gone, 1924

Sarah Stein has purchased your Issy Dog painting (*Tea in the Garden*, as they call it), and Doucet buys *Goldfish and Palette*, but shortly afterward, Doucet retires from Bernheim-Jeune and the Steins sell their collection to a dealer in Copenhagen.

With Shchukin no longer collecting your work, (he avoids you on the streets in Paris or Nice), you suddenly find yourself at fifty-four without collectors; all your early work is held outside of France. You shun dealers; the dealers are all out for their own profits, you are convinced. Who will buy your work? How will you live now?

Marguerite Marries Georges Duhuit, 1924

You don't want her to marry this man: it's simple, you don't like him. You suspect him. Is he good enough? Of course not. Is he creepily sycophantic and obsequious toward you? Yes. The glorious Marguerite, who has endured so much, who is so brave and smart, she must have an equal to her tenacity, her intelligence, her courage. Not this man. Not a man who cares more about furthering his career through you, her father, than he cares for Marguerite herself.

When he comes to visit you in Nice, sits in your brown chair in the studio, where Henriette brings him tea. He wants to promote your work, he wants to write about you, shocking things; he wants to cause a scandal. He wants, he wants, he wants. But it does not seem to be Marguerite whom he wants, but rather, proximity to you.

You don't like it. No, you don't like it at all.

France, The Nation, 1924

Postwar, even seven years out, your country is always patriotic; this can be counted on. So, it follows they would buy your *Odalisque in Red* now, their first Matisse canvas.

You try not to expect too much, but here is a man, who expects everything, and wants even more than everything, for surely there is something else beyond this struggle, this striving for the perfect line, the most saturated color, the teetering balance of composition, poised at the edge between tension and rest.

If you sell your new canvases, as you do now, the critics pan you. Your early canvases, praised as iconoclastic and Fauve, (he didn't mean it to become a tag, a name, a brand), this work does not sell, the gallery owners say it makes the collectors uncomfortable.

Though you are content to please no one but yourself, still, it rankles.

Your *Odalisque in Red*, finished a few years back, is boldly frank in its backlying, hands behind head, display. No woman would lie in such a way unless she were alone; so, since no one is supposed to be watching, viewer becomes voyeur. You've always been forced into this role of voyeur, in order to draw from the model. Since everything is alive to you, even drawing a landscape, or the room, or the view out the window, you feel yourself a voyeur.

As a result, you find it a stroke of evil genius to inflict this voyeurism on the viewer. In addition, you have brought the lesson of Renoir's studio into the canvas, and eliminated background: there is only one plane – the present. The woman lying on a gold divan above a red floor, in her burgundy ballooning pants, her gauzy shirt open, her torso, belly and breasts, exposed, the blue, circle-bordered exes of the screen behind her, cutting off the depth of field.

And so, you let them have it. Let them take the new work, frightened of the earlier work. Let them be the voyeur.

That Pesky Myth About Reality – Again

We misunderstand Egyptian art. We misunderstand the Minoans. They were striving for style, truth, beauty, emotion, power -- not realism. Realism didn't begin in earnest until Classical Greece because the ancients didn't want realism.

Let's face it, most artists don't value reality over truth or beauty or emotional power. When you listen to Erik Satie, do you say, is that realistic? When you watch Don Quixote tilt at windmills, do you say, Is that realistic? When you listen with Odysseus to the Sirens, and strap yourself to the mast so you won't be carried away by their song, *is that realistic?*

Realism is an ugly stain on the artistic landscape, that started in the mid-nineteenth century with Industrialism and should have ended in the Belle Epoque, when Art Nouveau, Decadence, and Impressionism tried to scrub it out.

Pierre Buys a Bugatti, January 1928

What greater way to celebrate the success of *The Moroccans* retrospective exhibit at your son Pierre's gallery in Manhattan than to buy a Bugatti? Low to the ground, oblong, tires way out in front – revealing the fragile undercarriage, its hood tied down with leather straps. Of course, you wouldn't celebrate this way, but your son Pierre has. He has purchased the horsey, elongated, fast racing car.

You don't like them, cars. They are too loud, too fast. Unlike a train, someone you are with has to drive it, and there are so many other things on the road: people, carts, horses. Someone could get hit, killed: the engine's noisy jangling like a rallying cry, Pierre driving too fast.

You're ambivalent about this century's machines. Use them, yes, but don't bow down to them. Don't worship them. Don't fetishize them.

Woman with Veil, 1929 (Saying Goodbye to Henriette)

You would have given up your wife for her, this model with whom you had worked so intimately for so long. But in the end, you gave her up to preserve her health, and later, when she married a schoolteacher and had a daughter, you painted her as well.

You are not good with loss. Loss of collectors, like Shchukin, who passes you on the street in Nice now, without even turning his head looking at you, as if you are a stranger. Loss of paintings to the Germans and Soviets during after the Great War. Loss of gallery owners. Loss of your pets: dogs, cats, doves. Loss of models.

But Henriette was not just a model. Even your wife insisted you part with her, and adamantly, you refused. It didn't matter if you shared a bed or not (and no one ever knew, you kept your affairs of the heart so private), but your wife Amélie knew that through Henriette she had lost you, lost your presence in her life, your devotion, your closeness, your thoughts, your attentions. Now they were all with her.

And when you let Henrietta go, it was for her health, not for your wife.

How do you paint the last portrait of a woman whose heart breaks with yours? A woman for whom you want the world, an acting career, Hollywood? A woman you ultimately failed (you feel), because you could not give her back her health, you could not give her the film career she wanted. You could only help her daughter, sixteen years later.

So when you paint her, for the first time, the checks that are usually on the floor are on her dress, and the background that is usually filled with flowers or paisleys or stripes, or all three, is a murky swirl of mostly solid red, green and blue colors.

Her forehead, below her black hair, is chore, her eyes veiled. Her expression chin-resting-on-hand resigned, but also angry.

You don't believe you will love someone like this again, work this closely, this intimately with a woman you love again. You are sixty, and you ache with fatigue, with age, with longing that all artists feed on.

You don't yet know that Lydia will come, at the end, to guide you through it.

Steichen photographs You in Manhattan, March 1929

You don't want to go. But when you arrive, that frantic energy mesmerizes you. You love Manhattan instantly.

Your son Pierre is your host in this frenetic city. He introduces you to the reaching skyscrapers, to the impoverished artists' studios, to the rivers on either side of Manhattan, cradling her like arms; he takes you to the galleries where they show the incomprehensible artists, to the new Metropolitan museum trying so hard to be like the Louvre; he takes you to parties where you are the guest of honor, to newspaper and magazine interviews, to energetic plays in Harlem and a singularly horrible area in mid-town called the broad way. Your son Pierre even drives you through traffic jams and feeds you an ice cream soda. In short (and except for the broad way), life is enchanting.

Forget Chicago, forget California, forget Tahiti: here is a world whose energy and absurdity matches your own. Why leave? Suddenly you wish more than ever that you were a young man and could start over again in New York. Young. Fresh start. Isn't that what everyone wishes for, in the last third of their life, when aches and remorse have set in? When you know you have botched everything? Begin again?

Too old? Yes, you convince yourself that starting out in Manhattan is for another life, a young life, in this case Pierre's. And so, reluctantly, regretfully, to Chicago.

But before you go, Pierre takes you to be photographed.

Steichen, the American ex-military man who, before the Great War, photographed Rodin's *Balzac* by moonlight, and who now takes photographs for the American glossy, full-of-pictures, how-we-should-live-now magazines, wants to take your picture for *Vogue. Vogue!* Do they know it's a French word? The layers of absurdity amuse you.

He is a tall man, but skinny. He is intense and bearded like yourself, but younger, his hair and beard darker. Only rarely are you on the other end of the gaze, are you on view, are you scrutinized. Usually you are staring in a white heat at your model to create the image. But now, he is staring at you through layers and layers of glass, in a big square machine on a tripod. This irony: you slowly grow to like it, perhaps.

He employs all the tricks: sits you sideways in the chair, leans you forward, as they do, your arms wrapped around each other and resting on the chair arm. He bends your head down, and slightly to the left so you must look up at his reflecting machine. Backlit, the shadow of your beard falls on your left shoulder. The mesh caning of the chair repeats the mesh of lit windows in the tall buildings behind you.

But you have tricks of your own: your suit jacket shows a subtle stripe from the texture of the fabric. Your stern expression reveals nothing: you will not let him in. You will play the Great Master, a thing you usually dismiss as childish.

But you do like him, for some reason unknown to yourself (perhaps his artisan skill, his hard work?), so you glare at him, through your glasses, to show you are just as intense, just as serious, just as driven, and more of a genius. He glares back, through his glasses, and through the many glass-prismed lenses of his camera, until you hear the faint click, clicks of satisfaction, like a rabbit gnawing on a carrot. A collaboration of mistrust.

Two Days in Los Angeles, 1929

After Chicago, you have two days to spend in this: the desert version of your own French coastline, so you go inland instead, to the oldest part of Los Angeles: Pasadena – where the rich live in their elaborate houses, perched on rolling hills, surrounded by their even more elaborate gardens: palm, yucca, wisteria, gardenia, jasmine, bougainvillea, lemon and orange trees, thick clipped green lawns – and above, endless sky, glitzy stars.

The secret you learn about Pasadena is, everything looks modest, almost plain. It is not decorated like a wedding cake – the accusation most often hurled at your coast. But if you look closer, the materials that make the houses are the highest quality, the landscaping the best design, and the combination, nestled in the hills, is beyond value – no one can afford its riches.

Here are the oldest, richest families, the art patrons, everyone, huddled in their enclave of serene gardens, like a page out of Scheherazade's *A Thousand and One Nights*. The water for these gardens is rumored to be stolen from the northern region of the state. The automobiles are the biggest and the most lemon yellow and metallic blue you have ever seen. Hollywood is just over the hill. They make the movies there.

You have two nights, and you spent them looking up: the view to the stars is clearer than you could have imagined.

Fakarava, 1929

When you visit a strange new country, across two oceans (or one large continent if you go in the opposite direction), it is always wise and cautious to have a guide, who is at least as educated as you, speaks your language, is well read, loves the arts, is half French, smells like vanilla, and is beautiful. If you are a painter, it helps if your guide can not only show you the new country, but embody the new country with her beauty.

You cannot paint now. To paint requires focus on nothing else, it would be to ignore this strange and unusually beautiful sea of islands all around you. So instead, you choose to sketch a few idle line drawings, and to immerse yourself totally in this new, magical place.

You thought your southern coast beautiful, but this is a different kind of beauty. The guava and mangosteen are richer. The scents of plumbago heavier, the shape and lie of the lotus cleaner. The air is thicker. The light is a quicksilver sheen. Their lighthouses rise stepped in stone like an Aztec temple.

The people are beautiful in a healthier, more sensual way. But they are not sexual. They are too much the land and the sky and the water. The Americans you think try to sexualize them, with their movies and their own perverted lusts. But these people cannot be simplified or made tawdry. They are too kind.

The blues of sky and sea on the coral rimmed atoll of Fakarava almost approach your only blue. The atoll proves that paradise did once flourish on earth, and that we should not have brought any of our beliefs or ideas here: not Christianity, not commerce, not our language, nor our boats, bicycles, raised beds, nor our syphilis, nor our rats and cockroaches.

Here you are the happiest of your life. Your four days here, like your signature stripe on the golden mean of your life, will last the rest of that life. Here you float in the lagoon, hanging on to the bending palm frond that touches the water. Here you make a companion of a runty dog. He is tawny, and short haired, and runs all over you as if your body belongs to him. As if you belong to him. He yaps and commands you. He smiles and barks, chasing after you.

At night your beautiful guide (whose close friend has given you access to the island) talks with you about philosophy, about ways to live with a quiet mind, about the blue colors and how they soothe and comfort you. You gaze at her skin in the firelight. You think how chaste and perfect this is. The perfect island: mouth of a volcano, the perfect woman, the perfect lime white of a vanilla flower, curves of its petals, broken open – the taste and scents of its mahogany pod; shapes and shadows of the firelight against her cinnamon skin.

You soak in the memories and the different colors of cerulean lagoon, verdigris leaves, vermillion hibiscus petals, and keep them forever close, never saying or drawing or painting anything about them, until the end of your life, when the saturated sheets of color find your scissors, and the memories come to your hand in a rush.

The Day After the Wall Street Crash, 25 October 1929,

you are in your painting studio, with colors, brushes, canvases, fabrics all around, sofas and divans, thinking about the vagaries and fragilities of the world. But you already knew about them. You worried about your collections when the Great War broke out, Shchukin's collection taken from his mansion by foot soldiers in the Russian Revolutionary Army, and you think about it now. If that United States of America would only have some sense, and their Wall Street Brokers realize that the money they embezzle affects the whole world. But no.

Your son Pierre tells you not to panic like everyone else. He tells you that every time you feel afraid, you should find one painting, just one painting you would be willing to sell. That's all. Then you will feel calm again.

You look around your studio, at the paintings of views out the studio window, paintings of the studio itself, paintings of models reclining on divans in harem pants and long, violet –striped robes, their elbows propped up. why does no one but you see the irony in this?

Sell them all! you think, but it does not make you feel calm, rather it ratchets up your anxiety even higher. You look out the window of your studio. The bay is calm. The tourists scatter in all directions, waving their morning newspaper, shouting at impassive waiters for their café Americain.

This bay, its water, and working, being present in the work, are the only things that can calm you. Because the work is all that matters. You've been penniless before; of course, you know it is more difficult to be destitute again, especially with daughters who need health care to simply breathe, sons who need help to find their start in life – a gallery? a military career? – wives who need safety and comfort of a house in the Paris suburbs, and an oversized, floppy, kindly, Issy dog.

You need to work. That is all.

The Other Sister, December 1929

The Claribel Cone collection, as substantial and important as Shchuckin's or Barnes', at Claribel's sudden and unexpected death, is now owned by the Etta: the other sister, the retiring sister, the sister who stood behind, in shadow, while her doctor/sister Claribel made deals, hostessed salons, dared, challenged.

Etta cajoled, apologized, smiled wryly, shook her head in resignation.

What will you say to her? How will you reassure her? What will convince her she can and also must step forward now, come into her own, as they say in America now, claim her ownership to this vast beloved collection of Matisse paintings?

Now Etta will take the lead; she will be solo; the bump and roll of the Baltimore social register will be hers to ride alone. How do you instill confidence? How do you make a not doctor, not collector/sister who has been left behind realize her value? Her worth?

You imagine Etta saying goodbye to sister/doctor Claribel in her adjoining apartment: *Claribel, don't leave me here all alone. I've always thought of us as a unit: The Two Sisters. The Cone Sisters.*

Two sisters: now Etta is sister to no one, and she is the art patron, Baltimore society hostess, art collector, in her own right. She must claim those rights.

But Claribel is already gone. The two, heady, eighth-floor apartments, filled with paintings, brimming over into the bathrooms, onto the closet doors, sculptures in the kitchens. It doesn't matter now that Claribel, the doctor/sister, the early lover of Gertrude, bought your first *Blue Nude*.

In a moment of evil genius, you devise a plan: a final portrait of doctor/sister Claribel, now that she's gone. Let the sittings, time together, work together forge a friendship with this Etta sister left behind.

Your secret? (For you always have one): It's Etta whom you love. It's Etta who reminds you of yourself, with her uncertainty, her self-doubt.

And so, you become friends, by working together. In these two adjoining apartments, and third above, you love the contrast of the nineteenth century heavy, curly, mahogany furniture, with the twentieth century paintings. The energy of paintings zings back and forth across the walls, so bright, so womanish, that you must open a window. You are used to bigger spaces, fewer works facing outward to the air. In your studio your paintings are stacked like rolodex cards. You don't see so many. You don't see them all. How can she absorb such energy?

Barnes Mural: *The Dance*, 1930

Your largest American collector, an important museum, important collection of Barnes' contemporaries, so you paint his two-story wall. Arched in front, glass doors behind. Foliage beyond the glass. And above? Tucked inside the arches? Dancers, of course. The ring of dancers that started in *Bonheur*, and have resurfaced, re-appeared in Shchukin's house in green with red men; now again they appear in blue with pink sexless creatures; always naked but always sexless, hairless. They appear again with a stool from the studio, as if part of a dream. They circle in space, around the stool, the stool perhaps supports a vase of flowers.

Now the dancers will reappear, gigantic, enormous, beyond the size of life, for they are outside of life, above our heads, to a museum no one is allowed to see, not even you, a private museum. A secret museum! The dancers will be fragmented, reaching across the arches to complete themselves, to each other. They will be gray on a background of alternating cornflower and pink, with the signature black lines. The reflection from the glass doors? From the foliage outside? And what of that? Curtains?

There will be airplane flights, trips to Meridien PA and back again to Nice. There will be yelling and arguments. There will be bent arm gestures, and renunciation, curses and giving up.

Maybe he lets you see the secret museum. Hidden from the public. Maybe he lets you see what is rumored to be the finest art collection in America (after Gertrude and Leo) of paintings by your predecessors, and contemporaries. Post Impressionists, Gauguin, Cezanne, Degas, Bonnard, and your Fauves. The Fauves you left behind, unwilling to stop experimenting. Unwilling to stop moving toward pure line, pure color, balance of the two.

So, the American visionaries multiply. First the siblings: Gertrude and Leo Stein. Etta and Claribel Cone. Now, the iconoclast, Barnes. (You, literal minded, picture minded, think of a red barn in a yellow field of blue flax.)

So, you try again. There are more arguments, because you are barred from the site. When you are let in again, the measurements for your mural are wrong, and so you have to start over from the beginning.

Eventually when the beautiful pink dancers hover under the arches, on a sometimes grey, sometimes blue background, with your signature black stripe and outlines; you will not gain entry to see them, nor to witness their reception. You will not be granted permission to loan them to other museums. No one can view them but Barnes. It is a secret museum. Even Shchukin is proud, has visitors, loans out his Matisses.

But not Barnes.

The Bamboo Stick, 1930

The Dance for Barnes is a mural, not a painting – and you are too old and careful for your dignity to clamber around on scaffolding. Standing only on a bench, you sway a brush at the end of a long bamboo pole. Like a conductor, you wield it, standing apart from your symphony of bodies in motion, half hidden under arcs like moons that the arches of the walls will make.

But you like restrictions. Though it's new, you like the idea of bodies half hidden, only suggested – like a secret. Although it's strange, you like the bodies five or eight times larger than a real human arm or leg or torso. This way you can celebrate the curves, the movement, the tension between bodies, among limbs, while you stand apart, orchestrating, wielding your bamboo pole, lighter than light, just a suggestion of heft so you know how to move it. Subtle, subtle, you are now a Mandarin, a sage, calligrapher, imparting wisdom from a mountaintop to those who will never see it.

Separate, removed, distant, the way you've always wanted to be, the way you've always imagined yourself, your intensity pushing you away from the world while you yearn for closeness, this tension, forever present in your work. Now it is displayed, wildly gargantuan-sized but not flamboyant, never that. How to create subtlety in such a large space, format? Only the master knows how: it's the tensions, the relationships, the movements that are subtle, what to choose, what to show and what to conceal. That is subtle in any size. The grand flourish is not welcome here. This is not the theater of the grotesque.

Wobbly, standing astride on your bench, feet shoulder-width apart, like a conqueror, like Napoleon before his fall – you dance the brush: your arms move in arabesques like the dancers themselves, their limbs the sway of overhanging leaves in a breeze, the rhythm of ripples in a lake, of water lapping, a swallow swirling for its own pleasure, trying out its wings.

Not a revelation – this mural making/music making – not your calling, like Puvis de Chavannes or Diego Rivera, but you will wield the bamboo pole again – at the chapel in Vence, from your bed after surgery – your walls will become murals: you will know what to do.

PART THREE:
SATURATE COLOR

To Padua to Revisit the Giottos, 1930

Stalled in creating *The Dance*, the deep blue Giottos of Padua that saved you as a Fauve – you need them to save you again, so you journey back to the Scrovegni Chapel in Padua, but not back to the past.

Immense color, vermillion Christ against his mauve violet betrayer, the betrayer's kiss, always gold, vermillion, mauve, the occasional splash of sea-foam green. Tension constructs the faces* in kiss, as Plato said, each face is for the other face.

But most important, the deep blues, deeper than any sky. The lighter blues grey-washed and transcendent. The greenish blues, water has become sky, sea has become sky.

The folds of robes. Always the robes. So many robes, so many angels, so many betrayers.

This is what you need; oddly, this vermillion-robed betrayer's kiss makes your hope return.

You see them as you are now, not as you were – a man in your forties. Now, in your sixties, you see something else, a different salvation, but an equally efficacious one: saturation of color, purity of line, arabesque – the perfection of each, the balance of all three in a single composition.

Three Difficult Men: Diaghilev, Shchukin, Barnes

Two are Russian and the other American. Of course. Could it be otherwise?

Are all collectors, museum owners and ballet impresarios difficult? Probably. They all wanted the best. Isn't the best difficult?

Diaghilev knew he could make his ballet company into the best in the world. He thought it was already. He wanted to astound. He chose the artists he considered the best in the world, so of course you were flattered to be asked. He knew enough about quality to let the choreographers and composers take the lead when making decisions about the dance movements and the musical score. Get the best people and let them do their work. But otherwise he made stubborn decisions, knew he was right, everyone else go to hell. And they did. He thought nothing of ruining an entire life of a dancer. He was at war with the philistines, the common, the ugly, the boring the regular, the mundane, the not-art. He was righteous.

With poets, dancers, composers working for him he might be ruthless, but with the art patrons he could be charming, even lovely. He pretended to concede to them, without losing his dignity or his stature as the great man. If you crossed him, he would ruin your life. You'd end up in an asylum for the insane, or worse.

Barnes, on the other hand, railed at the world, felt victimized while he kept the Americans out, excluded them from viewing his private collection. He wanted to be an educator, not a collector. He wanted to show the collection in groupings, in context, not the way a museum would show them. For this he was ridiculed, then scorned, then sued. He was pugnacious and fought back. Meridien, Pennsylvania became a battleground for the right to view art.

Shchukin, was the only real victim, when he was made tour guide to his own collection, and groundskeeper to his own great mansion. But that is what revolutions do, yes: if not beheaded or shot, the rich become the servants, and the rebels become the tyrants. He was a man born fifty years too soon to be a collector of this radical art.

Portraits of the Studios: Herself Surprised*

The studio becomes a portrait. Portrait of the studio. Self-portrait. Red studio the most famous, flaming red, studio on fire, little paintings cover the right back wall, popping out pink, gray, slate blue, more stacked in ochre and light grey against the orange mirror, a giant violet figure painting to the far left; a curvy white chair, a white and a black sculpture sit side by side on their respective stools; the stove, the bureau; on a table a white plate, a box of charcoal pencils, a black vase (is it a hookah?), a wine glass.

In the next portrait, the studio turns dark, with its brown carpet with purple flowers, it's sienna divan, a screen draped with teal fabric topped with sky blue swirls, a mirror to the left reflecting that teal, a window to the right drawing the eye out to a lighter green, citrine, and the same sienna of the divan and sky blue of the swirls. Above the screen: squares with colors and a grid.

Finally, the puce studio, striped walls, a posing figure, paintings of figures against the wall, a screen with a black drapery with brown flowers, and a green drapery with lighter brown, smaller flowers. Tiny red stool in front. The large puce gridded window with the dark green palm leaves outside, the dark red table with splayed legs, the brick red floor.

To the left, black sculpture stands on a stool; an easel supports a sculpture of a knee-bent, elbow-bent, almost-seated figure; a large painting of sienna figures on dark moss green background hangs between but above the sculpture and screen; a bordered brown rug sits below. A small chest hides behind the half-seated sculpture's stool.

Studio portrait. Self-portrait. Studio as reclining woman, as seated woman, as standing woman, as posing woman. Studio as herself surprised. Studio in which you constantly surprise yourself. Studio as delight. Surprise and delight. With view. Room with a view.*

Deliberately flattening the studio, using pattern. Depth erased. Foreground eliminated: until all is background. Flat and square, like a postage stamp. You have done this.

Dance Cutouts, 1932

Because the dancers must come back, as they should. It's only been three years. Now they are cut out, not painted on. The color is soaked into the paper, and then the richly colored paper is cut into shapes. Better than painting. So incisive. Yes, a pun. Matisse humor. The shapes run like a river, curve like Tahitian seaweed, like philodendron leaves, like doves, setting the field for pure blocks of color, what you always wanted, no, just pure color. The Color in dreams. The original color, not just pure: it's saturated, intense, so intense, in a hundred years it will be made waterproof from its intensity. And unbreakable. But now you carve it with scissors. The dancers come back, they dance in lines around the large studio, high on the wall. They encircle you. You are the center. You are happy to be back. Happy they are back, I mean.

Nice is A Fishbowl*

You've painted many fishbowls. You place them in lovely seaside rooms, with colorful paisley and striped wallpaper and curtains, balconies, a view of the bay beyond, with its wooden sailboats rocking in the water, and on sand, its striped red umbrellas and languishing sunburned bathers.

But now, do you see glass walls are curving up around you? Hemming you in? Are you contained in a concave layer of glass? Is the studio that once set you free and connected you to the world enshrouding you in glass?

You live for twenty years in a ten-block radius of your studio. This is your fishbowl. You have everything you need, a green grocer, a view. You have supplies and models sent in. Collectors also arrive. Once you needed to go back to Paris to change studios or see shows mounted, or to Issy, to visit your daughter and pet your Issy dog. You once needed to travel an hour away to see the Master Renoir.

But all that is in the past. Everything comes to you, and the glass grows thicker, curves in tighter, refracts more light. Soon, in Cimiez, you will not need to leave the studio at all. Then you will not be able to. You trusted your work to save you, but it tricked you and now it traps you. But you can still see the bay.

Pull Yourself Out of Boredom*

Being stalled in your work is not the same as being bored, but it can cultivate boredom, breed boredom. Some say boredom is necessary. You have never been bored. Frustrated, maybe – angry, restless. Of course, full of longing. They say artists feed on longing, on desire. Yours is the desire for harmony among perfect line, balanced composition, and deep, saturated color. It is not as simple as it sounds though, is it?

When you are restless you take a trip – to Padua, to Tahiti, to Morocco, for example. When you were angry, you visited Renoir to learn grace from the master, and after he was gone you abandoned grace and just yelled at work men, delivery boys, grocers, shopkeepers. Never your models or assistants.

When you are frustrated you draw the landscapes, especially through the windows. You paint the goldfish trapped in bowls, though they can see through the window to the outside. But there is no fresh water there. The cat's paw poised at the top of the fishbowl, ready to scoop out the fish; the curved glass refracting the bright incandescent light of southern, coastal France you love so much.

When you are filled with longing you paint or sculpt from the model, or draw from her, even better to draw, the swift curved lines matching the fleeting aches in your rib bones and collar bone. When you are filled with desire you drape the divan with jacquard and paisley prints, drape the screen with check prints, drape the table with a floral print, tack the Escher-like geometries of tapa printed bark-cloth or kuba cloth on the walls before you position your model. You give her more instruction than usual. You ask her to change position frequently. She goes to the window, beyond the goldfish bowl, and looks out at the bay. Her longing matches your own. Her desire is to work in the theater, or dance for Diaghilev, or work in a designer shop, or paint like a master. Your desire and hers fuse; she finds the perfect pose. She can keep still under your gaze for hours. Few can match her poise.

So: anger, restlessness, fatigue even, desire and longing – but never boredom.

Saint-Jean-Cap-Ferrat, 1934

All the blues are here: the indigo and aqua blues of the sea (ultramarine when the weather is cloudy), the gray-washed cornflower blue of the sky, royal blue stripes of umbrellas, turquoise blue stripes on boats, cerulean stripes of awnings, lapis of mosaics, Egyptian blue of a vase in a display window, Blue of Genoa in tourists' jeans, azure of water in a glass, malachite of the water in fountains at the so-many villas.

This should give you rest: but what if there is no rest? What if you've extended yourself to the limit? Do you take two weeks, two months maybe, and just look at the colors of the bay and boats, the sky, the leaves moving in the wind; listen to birds, to children laughing; feel the breeze, feel the sun on your arms and neck. You do this until the pressure is unbearable and you cannot "rest" anymore. You do this until you see canvases painting themselves, even though you've not painted on an easel in five years.

Illustrations for Joyce's *Ulysses*, March-September 1934

The illustrations are for Joyce's *Ulysses*, but you know Homer's, so you work from his, which is of course, unsatisfactory to the author, who tells you so, when you meet with him. Still, you do not read the Joyce book, but instead, stubbornly, re-read Homer. You mean to break through to a new way of seeing, but words, words to you remain the same across the centuries, or worse, they disintegrate, so, and the older the better.

Nausicaa, Penelope, Circe, the Sirens, Calypso – except for Cyclops they give you only wind, false voices and women to draw – dangerous women, seductive women, so seductive you must tie yourself to the mast; scheming women, charming women, entrapping women, imprisoning women, feasting women, magical women, but also helpful women, advising women, and then there is Penelope, so ambivalent, pulling out the thread of her weaving every night, as you do on your canvas, but nevertheless conducting a trial of the suitors – just in case her husband does not come home.

Aeolus, the wind god, can batter anyone's boat, and rightly, when you are working on him: the publisher complains, Joyce is worried, you must read his text, you must see Dublin, you must meet with Joyce in Paris because this is not Homer, this is something new.

But you must focus, despite the winds, the tides, the batterings, and when you finish with this windy god you blind Cyclops, drawing and redrawing the maiming, because now you are Hercules, now you are strong, now you are determined that no contemporary text will come between you and the ancients, you and the gods, you and the sirens, the pigs, the islands brighter, windier, dryer even than Nice or memory.

Hercules' embrace is a crushing death: you are inspired by Pollaiuolo's exquisite drawing, as Rodin was, for one of the sea of bodies embracing on his *Gates of Hell*. So you draw it, over and over, smaller and smaller, until the voices stop, the demands stop, everyone and every thing is at bay; until just you and your pencil, paper, and this drawing remain, the movements of your arm and hand, dusty charcoal, the rustling paper, the fluttering of dove wings, outside the window the crackle of passersby, roasting cinders of chestnut, filling up your head, the studio, the world.

"Unless the work is going to save me," Matisse to Pierre, September 1935

Unless the work is going to save you, you can't work. No one else understands this logic, but they do not wake with your panic, do not panic when they leave the house, leave the street, leave the neighborhood. They do not panic when they worry. Perhaps they do not even worry.

Pierre looks at you with dismay. You've survived utter poverty, destitution, working from a closet studio, you've survived all the greatness at the beginning of the twentieth century: the Great War, your daughter's constant medical emergencies, the Great Depression; you've survived being ridiculed, snubbed, ostracized, you've survived saying goodbye to a work you've struggled with for ten years – never to see it again, you've survived your work being stolen by revolutionaries, and

seeing great collectors turned into tour guides at their own mansions –
and yet now, when you are past all that, you now panic. Why?

Because you are getting older. Because you have just started
painting again after not painting on an easel for six years. Because you
are ill. Because you are too intense and have exhausted your reserves of
will and focus. Because you still have not found the pure line, saturated
color and balanced composition you are looking for, all in one painting,
perfect.

You've only found perfection in this southern French light,
in everything on Fakarava, and perhaps, now, in Lydia. But even
perfection won't make you calm – only work. Work, companionship,
collaboration. This will calm you.

The Blue Eyes, 1935

Lydia Delectorskaya was going to be a doctor, but she could not afford
the Sorbonne Medical School, into which she'd been accepted. So, she
ran off with a handsome Russian Officer, who lost his fortune gambling
at the Monte Carlo casino wheels – and grace being to god – she ended
up helping you. Otherwise, you think you certainly would be dead and
gone by now. Dead and buried. Dead, and you fear: quite forgotten.

At first, she takes care of Mme Matisse. She does not pose. Then
it slowly begins: she opens windows, feeds doves, answers the door,
the phone, keeps distractions at bay. She cooks and cleans. Then she
organizes your work, catalogues and makes notations for each piece.
Next, she assigns work to assistants. She tells the delivery men where
to store supplies. She dresses and directs the models, drapes the screens
and divans with fabrics. Finally, she assists with museum curators and
collectors.

When at last she first sits down to pose, you paint her sullen, resting
her head in her arm, hiding her left cheek, her eyes sullen. You do not
make her beautiful, because she would be insulted. It would be a sign
of disrespect. You paint her in a navy striped tank, against a green and
yellow chair, behind that – a teal background with a burgundy stripe

and red splotch. You do justice only to her beautiful auburn hair, but it is the first time you have painted at the easel in six years, so you are simply grateful. Mme Matisse has fled; your behavior is insupportable; you have replaced her thirty years of working collaboration with another's.

Pink Nude, April-September 1935

You've been drawing steadily for six years – so long that now you feel bold, outrageous even. This bright, sickly pink is bold, but bolder still the black checks in the background, the pose of fake innocence, the pose of cynical seduction.

But it is not what you wanted, so you rub it out and try again: black checks becoming indigo, black bulb behind her becoming yellow, pink flesh transmutes to a muddy ochre, the beautiful face – so like Lydia's becoming blank, becoming somber, becoming stiff, becoming someone else entirely; while Lydia – fearful of your anger, confusing your intensity with distress – tells you stories of her childhood: the elk, the frozen tundra, the wooden houses, the only warmth coming from the fire in the house stove (which she did not say, but threatened to burn down the house), hunters returning with small game, frozen; milkmaids returning with milk, also frozen; everything frozen, except for your heart when you watch Lydia remember her childhood: the state and polytechnic universities that later made her set her heart on the University of Paris and Medical school, the third-generation exiles, finally: revolution, war, ceasefire, her doctor-father worn down administrative duties, then dead from typhus – the end of her childhood at eight years old.

You work six months, trying to synthesize your loud, sustained recent drawing experience with your lifelong knowledge of the complexities of color. When it is in progress, Bonnard sees the face blotched out and is frightened; but in June, when it is only a scratched in outline, and the color is yet to emerge, of all the canvases in the studio, your son Pierre goes to it immediately, whispering optimistic about the next step, the next stage, the end of harem pants, the demise of paisley draped-screens, of views out windows. Here there are no windows, only Lydia's eyes.

Grandson Claude – 1935

Three grandchildren, but it is Claude you hold in your arms; it is to Claude you show the doves – caged on the open veranda, to Claude you spout your philosophy – as if a five-year-old might understand. You believe he does. You can feel his little heart pounding in against your arm when you hold him.

He is small and kind, your Claude, he smiles weakly at you. Since you remember how you shied away from the strange grey skin, rotting teeth and decaying animal smells of your own grandparents, you are embarrassed to expose him to your old age when he is a tender new shoot on the family's orchid.

He watches intently when you draw, and when you start painting again, when you do cut outs to recreate the dance for Diaghilev's *Le Rouge et Noir* ballet. You have returned from Tahiti, but he looks at you as if you are an exotic sea creature, or as if you are both under water. Later, when you create the giant Oceania cut outs, he will like the view from underwater best.

He seems happiest when you take him down to the bay of Nice, with his orange bucket and his blue toy boat. He runs back and forth aimlessly, plays hide and seek with the incoming waves, dips his toes in, digs for crabs, inspects seaweed, chases birds.

Sometimes when you are immersed in work you will emerge to find him gazing over your shoulder, staring at the doves, or standing at the window looking out at the bay.

He is as special to you as one of your own children. When Claude is not with you, you are resigned to the choices you've made, to aging, to your partial success and to all those who misunderstand you. But when you are with him you long to be innocent again, young again, start over.

Other times you revel in his perfection: his small, unblemished hands, his unworn skin, his clear eyes, his silky hair, his shy but forthright manner, his curiosity, his focus, his openness. You know in some ways you must remain a child to create art, but the complications of the world make that impossible. When you are discouraged you call those complications sordid, or cruel. When you are working well you call them complexity, variation, you insist they are natural, organic.

The sun sets vermillion and pink around the end of the bay. Claude is napping now, his knees curled up to his chest, his elbows bent, hands near his face, face flushed, hair tousled. You wonder at his trust. You see him in his future, as a vibrant man, exuberant, immersed in life. You envy him.

Nymph and Faun, 1935-43

You start with line drawings, the voluptuous inks of Lydia on her back, smiling, her welcoming arms resting on her hips. Amélie and Marguerite are horrified, you cannot show them, you cannot sell them, they say; but you do show them in London where such things are understood, and they do sell.

You return to the worn-out theme of Faun and Nymph, but now it is different: he wants to enrapture, not trap, not force. You paint them into a giant eight by six-foot forest of citrine, deep greens and washed out lemon yellow, with an indigo-carmine forest path whispering by them. You do another, horizontal now, with beautiful grass greens and hunter greens, the carmine path creeping up onto a yellow stripe, indigo consigned to the edges now, the pink figures faded to flesh; but Amélie and Marguerite say you must smudge out the pink figures; it is obscene; it is the last betrayal; Amélie insists she will leave you. This is not a model, it is a collaboration, and Lydia has taken Amélie's place. However chaste it might or might not be in the studio, it is fulfilled on the canvas, and in your hearts, for you have revealed your deepest cares to her, and she to you.

Woman in Blue Dress, 1938

Flatten out the picture plane. Flatten. Swaths of color. Nothing to interrupt the eye. So only the curves show: the upward curve of the bright yellow sofa arm, like a swan: the exact complement of the downward curve of the white frills that cascade to the bottom of her dark blue dress and rest on the floor.

The black arcs etched with plaid sit complacent behind the red arcs etched with leaves: the sofa she's sitting on? Above her waist this red becomes a checked wall.

Faces on the wall, blue etched in white, yellow lined in black, seem to mock her: boredom on the blue face, amusement on the yellow face.

On her flesh colored face: an attentive, sophisticated stare, focused, perhaps angry.

Her loosely etched, raised left hand points a finger to her temple, like she *has a gun to her head*, as if she's been caught right at that moment in her story, a story told from model to painter.

Her right hand, resting on her cornflower dress, between the two downward spirals of white ruffles, is wrapped in rosary beads, black and white, like a penitent, or a contrite woman waiting to confess.

Directly behind her head, a floral arrangement in yellow and green, fans out behind her like an aura or a crown, or the back of an Elizabethan collar.

Who is this woman in blue? Why is she blue? Why is she flattened into the sofa and wall? Who are the faces mocking her? Why do they mock? Why does she have her hand/the gun to her head?

Is she the painter? Are the portraits behind mocking your exasperation? Are you praying for redemption? Relief? Appealing to a Catholic god for charity? for respite? for hope? for a solution?

Is spending your whole life trying to find pure line, pure color, and put them in balance, like holding a gun to your head? Is this our life? mine? yours?

The Regina, Cimiez, 1938

You think your abscess should not hurt, because another war is coming, but your mouth does hurt, so at your wife's insistence, Lydia takes you to Paris to see your dentist. Running parallel, (you see your life in parallels) you don't want to move, but your studio lease is up at Charles Felix so you are among the first to buy adjacent apartments at the Regina in Cimiez, in all its run down glory, its brief flight, like your birds, as the Excelsior-Regina Palace, lasting only twenty-five years or so, as the century turned, through to the beginning of the Great War. You don't want to take advantage of the war to profit by buying this apartment, but no one else will buy, (it will be another year before they do), so you are really helping the seller, others tell you.

On the way back to Nice from Paris, you and Lydia stop to buy your models six dresses, (Lydia chooses them), not knowing they will last through the coming war, and a little later, not knowing you would become estranged from your wife and daughter, then reunited with your daughter, over Lydia's companionship and your aloofness from the Resistance. A stain on your family record: you painted while your women fought in the Resistance. Replacing your working companion and wife Amélie, with your chaste working companion Lydia.

No, it's not only or even primarily about sex, it's much worse than sex, it's companionship, and much worse than just companionship, it's an artist's working collaboration, for slowly, Lydia has gone from taking care of Amélie, and a few of your immediate needs, to becoming your administrative assistant in everything you do, plus: studio assistant, model, supervisor of the other models, costume manager, archivist, liaison to collectors, curators, and any other buyers, dovecote keeper, housekeeper, cook, canvas stretcher, as well as the woman who asks you why you are upset, and brings you your chamomile tea. Soon she will be pinning cut outs for *Le Rouge et Le Noir*, because you can't say no to Massine.

La Rouge et Noir, ballet, 1938-39

You will never see your mural *La Danse* again, (nor will anyone else), so you agree to redo it for Diaghilev. It's been twenty years since you helped them with robes for *The Nightingale*, and even though you vowed never to work with Diaghilev again, even though you won't admit it to anyone, you miss being around the geniuses fighting, and the dancers scuttling across the stage. You watch Massine's dancers: they are not interpreting the Shostakovich music; no, it is the reverse: they obey the choreography, but they are the main drivers of this dancing play. This is as it should be, you say. You say this to everything, resigned acceptance, except to your periods of despair and panic when you are stalled in your work.

You recreate Barnes' arches on stage, you imprint leaf forms like tentative, clutching fingers on the dancers' leotards, then watch your mural come alive through the sway, jump, stretch, lean, arc and curve of the dancers.

For the curtain: indigo, bone white and lemon cut outs, with a black Icarus falling, or a flame thrower arching his back.

***

Massine likes to mount ballets based on symphonic music. This is his last, and his most absolute, or that is, in retrospect, what all the critics will say of him.

Your curtain with its Icarus, its flame thrower, is riotous, your leafy yellow-green leotards on the dancers subdued, but accentuating their movements, following them, as if leaves were falling and swaying in the wind, swirling around them as they dance.

The Monte Carlo crowd is among the richest and most decadent in Europe, so their sensibilities cannot be offended by the ultra modern. They are not afraid of what they don't understand. Protected by their wealth, like children, they have the luxury of being curious. They are required to be sophisticated, and Shostakovich, Massine, Diaghilev, the Ballets Russe are among the most sophisticated composers, choreographers, empresarios and players of all Europe.

You count yourself a minor player in this scene, and simply enjoy fast and slow, loud and soft, blasty and fluty orchestration, the beautiful movements and collaborations of the dancers, the enhancements your work has made to the ballet. It is indeed a collaboration, in which you have played a minor part, you think, but a beneficial one. It is good. In Paris in June they will be critical, they will rant and curse and growl. So, now is the time to enjoy, to be content, if just for an evening.

Le Chant, for Nelson Rockefeller, February 1939

To hang above the third-generation oil magnate Nelson Rockefeller's 810 Fifth Avenue fireplace mantle, the commissioned painting is itself framed in a fireplace mantle on the top and sides of the canvas, then cut around the actual fireplace mantle, below. Irony?

Is there irony as well in the two conversations? Above, one woman looks to the other, who looks away; below, one woman faces and reads to another, who sleeps on her arm. Charming, but why do both the women on the left face the women on the right, and why does the woman on the right either turn away or sleep?

Your signature line is drawn between the two women above – the right's background in navy, the left's background in grass green. These are in turn complimented by the women above's matching navy tops: shirt and shirt dress; and below, the reading woman's grass green dress. Only the sleeping woman blazes alone in a carmine sheath, though it in turn is reflected in a red chair above left, and red corner above right, shaping a subliminal triangle or cone.

They are all blonde, except for the auburn haired woman who reads; they are all pink fleshed, except for the sleeping, carmine sheathed woman, who is brighter. Is she more pink because she sleeps? Because the carmine reflects on her face?

Incongruous amongst this balanced composition of navys, grass greens and carmines, is the above right woman's cobalt-violet flowing skirt.

Is this his family? Or yours? Will the fireplace loungers be staring at their reflection in the portrait? Will they be confounded? Amused? Is it about the War? Is it about your own family? Your wife?

Paris – A Café at Gare St. Lazare, July 1939

The Montparnasse studio is empty. Issy is empty. The Regina studio on the high bluff in Nice is empty. But still, Amélie is enraged, frightening, manic even. She has been so for four months. Lydia's shooting herself in the collarbone and fleeing to her aunt's home outside Paris has not helped. The lawyers have given Amélie half of your work of forty years together: drawings, paintings, watercolors, sculptures, busts, fragments – but they cannot give your wife back your collaboration, which is what she wants, what you, so cruelly, have now transferred to Lydia.

No amount of pleading to Amélie that this collaboration with Lydia is chaste, that it is necessary for you, an old man now, to continue painting, none of it, calms her. She will have none of it. She will be young again and be your sole collaborator in art again, or she will be nothing. And being nothing, she will take half of the work you did together. Her or Lydia.

But you must keep Lydia. And so, you face down your wife's frightening rage.

You have never warmed to criticism, anger, rebuke. You have never laughed it off as others have. You have never countered with jokes, banter, seduction, suggestion, conciliation. In the face of this anger you are terrified, you sit silent, sullen, watching yourself withdraw. You find that you cannot raise your head; you can barely move your leg against the wrought iron chair, or lift your coffee cup. Even the waiter looks at you with alarm.

The Village Inn, Rochefort, September 1939

You have fled Paris with Lydia, and exhausted, have encamped at The Village Inn, while to the east, Hitler's army invades Poland.

Alone since March, when she shot herself and fled Nice, saying she'd been fired, Lydia is fragile and injured, frightened and bird-like. Not the Lydia you have come, slowly and carefully, to know. You must remake your bond. You must convince her, gently and tenderly, that you cannot work without her assistance. She has given up her dream of medicine, study, important work for you. And so you must trade that important work for assisting an artist.

The trouble: You do not think you are important. In fact, you fear you'll be lost to history within fifty years of your death, but you have only confided this to your daughter Marguerite. Your worst fear. Everyone has a worst fear.

You take walks together. You and Lydia, in the dying summer, you watch the leaves turn. You look up at the quaint grey-stone houses, with their high-pitched slate roofs, and wonder what life would be like if you were young again, or if it were over. You stop at a green-grocer stall, and finger the grapefruits, the asparagus, despite your hunger, wondering if you should paint a still life. You avoid the spa, eye contact, casual conversation. You walk along the quay and watch the boats rock in the silty river water. You want to follow that river the short distance west to the sea, and live again.

Eventually you ask her to continue to Nice with you, resume her duties. You cannot work without her. How do you say this? How does one say one's life depends on someone else, when all you can offer them is work, all you can say is relinquish your own doctor dreams, and instead, be of use to mine? Rescue me.

La Musique, September 1939

Dance without music? Rarely. Often, there has been music: Marguerite or Pierre at piano, music lessons, at rest in the salon. A piano lounging all curves in the salon, like an odalisque. A cubist head of a boy above a black piano in a gray and blue room. To the right of the window.

But now, when the background wall becomes giant, sky blue philodendron leaves on pitch black, it begins. The incised leaves. The cut-out looking leaves, which will become seaweed, which then become squiggles, which eventually become a philodendron-seaweed hybrid, and delight all who see them.

In front the woman holding the guitar stares out, right out at you the painter, and us the viewers, like Manet's staring girl from her divan. She is dressed in a cornflower blue slip of a long sleeved, V-neck dress, her hair is as black as the philo background, her features in the same black outline, her shoulders and breasts outlined the same. Her skin is pale but not peachy. She sits in a chair draped in a fiery red with white scratches, like mohair.

Next to her, a darker woman, in an ochre high neck dress, the same black outlines, but she looks away. She is seated on a black cushion, with the same scratches. A red tile design jumps out from behind her back.

On the seafoam-green table, sweet sounds of sheet music flutter, and a deep red mango, so seriously reclines. Below, hints of the red tile floor peek out between the table and blue dress, the table and sienna legs of the other woman, the woman who looks away.

You started it as a complimentary piece to Rockefeller's Song, but it has become something else entirely, hasn't it?

Bird Man, Nice, October 1939

With the Moroccans in the hallway, Lydia back to stay, and your studio empty of everything except what you now work on: you are the work in progress.

But next door: three hundred doves, and they are all yours. The Moroccans in the hallway make you drawings of giant mud-ochre bee hives, with square openings and sticks radiating out from the curved edges, saying: these are their ancient vernacular dovecotes. Impractical – too fragile if the Germans are really coming – but they are beautiful.

Hitler's armies have been through Czechoslovakia and Poland now; Paris is empty. Amélie is gone forever, too enraged, too bitter about his alleged betrayal he couldn't even look at her.

But the doves. A room full of doves. Think of it: all white, the fluttering. The sounds of flutter, of coo. Necks entwined.

Every day you stand in the dove room, subsumed by whiteness and flutter. Once you are calm, you take two or even three doves back to your studio to keep you company while you work. Every day the Bird Man comes and tends to them, so you don't have to worry.

As Lydia tends to the business of the studio, you needn't worry about that either. But she and the Bird Man cannot stop the war, cannot stop Amélie's frantic, menacing rage, so you still have sleepless nights, and when you do sleep, you still wake up screaming, sweaty, panicked. Birds notwithstanding.

You are the work in progress. You are Icarus – the Bird Man.

Lydia, October 1939 – *Young Woman in a Blue Blouse*

The first violet, a cobalt violet, so unstable, so expensive (thought to be derived from silver), that it has not been used in eighty years. But you buy it on the war's black market, for her so long of neck and face (or so I imagine). You want all the colors to be those of Antiquity, or if not that, the Renaissance: her deep celestial/ cerulean blue tidy blouse with its scalloped collar, the Egyptian (light) Blue sky, her cropped just above the shoulder ochre yellow hair, carmine (kermes, cochenille) red lips. You reach further back, to the Temple at Knossos, for the wavy bone black outlines of her hair, nose and eyes.

The expression in her eyes is mysterious, but mysterious like the Sphinx, not like the Mona Lisa. You want her ethereal, but at the same time, most definitely there. Solid, but with a mystery that's impenetrable, by charm or time, or art, or even by love. Even by a last love, that endures beyond health, beyond life, beyond usefulness.

She is angry. You fear you have nothing to give her. Her high forehead tilts back at the hairline. Her eyes are wide set, deep violet, and symmetrical. Her long nose is unnaturally narrow and almost touches her mouth. Her elephant ears flap asymmetrically. She is a beauty, but she is not perfection. Her neck is fantastically long, longer than the oval of her head. She is not perfection, but she is fantastic, and your longing for perfection is embodied in her. She is where western Europe meets eastern. She is a blonde Buryat monk. She is your ideal. Out of the reach of your old age, she is your dream, your daily companion, your help, your torturous solace.

The scallops and waves in her hair evoke a Greek sea, as do the solid long lines of her face, and the darker below and lighter above swaths of blues for blouse and sky. The prim scalloped collar of her blue blouse evokes a Parisian secretary or restaurant hostess. And yet, somehow, the painting is cohesive except for the ears, which seem to belong on a monkey or elephant. Whose ears are those? What head, what memory, what other artist's painting might they be from?

A feeling of straight lines hidden in the curves, hence the long neck, broad shoulders, the long nose ridge. A feeling of dark hidden in the blonde, hence the dark hair waves, the dark outlines, dark lips. A feeling of asymmetry embodied inside the symmetry, hence the mismatched ears, the eyes akimbo, the wider left lapel, the raised right shoulder. A feeling of red in the blues and yellows, hence the mouth.

Woman becomes blonde, assistant becomes model, model becomes companion. Portraits begin to smile, nudes lighten, foliage brightens; the artist's model: love, care; where love begins again, the end of life also begins, but work never stops.

You are seventy. You have fifteen years to live.

Roumanian Blouse, 1940

There's a war coming. You will not ignore it, but you will paint through it. You will not collaborate, but you will keep working. While you work, your daughter and estranged wife will fight for the Resistance.

The model in the Roumanian blouse, as much as she shows her neck, looks like your daughter Marguerite, who will be jailed, tortured, set free again as someone else entirely.

Maybe it is your only painting at this time with dull, earth colors: browns, ochres, siennas, blacks, a navy blue for the skirt. Perhaps it's your only painting of this time where the color is not saturated, and the canvas shows through it. Marguerite as a ghost of eastern Europe, the proud rebel of liberté, égalité, fraternité.

The only static painting: no movement, except perhaps in the raised left shoulder of the model. The hands are clasped together demurely. Yet the pattern in the Roumanian blouse yells: life, dancing, leaves, flowers, jumpy bees, a secret code, release from tyranny, at last freedom.

Still, the war is coming. Picasso has painted the *Guernica*, for Spain, for the rebel fighters, the resistance. You paint your doves.

But now, the blouse, two leaf-columns, to signify the breasts hidden below, to mark them. On the sleeves, tattooed designs, cross hatched ochre, and striped yellow, black squiggles. Because the war is coming. Longer, deadlier, cities turn to ash in your mouth. No one will see this as your war painting, your warning, even your reprimand.

On the girl's face, an astonishment of riches. On her Roumanian blouse, the patterns of celebration, dance, repetition, memory. Reddish brown and navy anomaly.

When we see the Roumanian blouse again, it's the same year, she is the dream, a sleeper, her pink face resting on her white bloused arm, on a yellow pillow, on a bright mauve wing chair, above an apple red floor. On the back of the blouse a patch of yellow with more sea-wave designs.

When we see her again, she is seated in a lemon yellow bergère chair, in seafoam harem pants, behind a seafoam cabinet. The chair dominates, the woman in the Roumanian blouse sinks into it. Behind her a mauve design, maybe a leafy plant, sways over her head, unbalancing the canvas, making her position in the room seem precarious at best. The navy blue carpet with white chevron patterns shimmers underneath the room. The amber vase to her right mimics the ochre bands on the upper arms of her blouse. She looks unhappy, discontent, even angry.

Black lines, 1940,

enter the frame, squiggling, moving, sleepers – the women are sleeping now, or perhaps they just pretend to sleep. Some who work in shops at night and model in the morning are tired enough to sleep. Some of the models are comfortable enough to sleep. Sideways on a divan that's been draped with a brightly patterned fabric. Sprawled in a chair festooned with a paisley shawl. Hunched over a table, covered with a floral table-cloth, in front of the window, elbows touching the goldfish bowl.

What is it about sleeping? Is it intimate? Is it secret? A Secret? Do you think it is special, requires trust? You sleep rarely now, as you get older. You will sleep less and less. this is something you have to look forward to.

In the meantime, the models sleep. Reclining on an elbow, in a confined space that becomes checkered with abstract squares, after the fact. Models enlarge, atomize, shrink, sleep on a settee in front of a screen, adorned with yet another patterned shawl, the settee also draped with floral, the floor also rugged by a tapa bark cloth etched with chevrons. It is dizzying, it is more Escher than what Escher will be. But still, they sleep.

Beyond the window, the sea air lulls them. You can almost smell the soft, salty tang. The billowy, clean, slightly moist air. Against the sand, the waves from the sea stretch themselves like cats onto the shore, making sleep-inducing whooshing sounds, so lovely, so silken, and relaxing, that sleep becomes inevitable. Back in the studio, your intensity is so impersonal, so consistent, so silent, that the models acclimate, so despite what for others might be discomfort of holding a position or being stared at, they can actually fall asleep.

The studio cats are calming; in the same way they calm racehorses at a stable, they calm models in the studio: their slinky movements, their slight brush of fur on the legs or arms as they pass by, their purr, the warmth of their bodies. So yes, the models sleep.

So, you watch, you work. The beauty denied, the quest for the fusion of pure line and pure color still beyond your reach, their youth denied, their languor denied, and also their peaceful sleep, all denied to you. Still, you work. You quest.

PART FOUR:
SYNTHESIZE LINE
AND COLOR

Le Réssuscité, The Risen, May 1941

Your beautiful dog Raudi has died, the song thrushes have died, the doves have been sold or fled in search of ant eggs, soldiers and refugees are dying. Pierre has returned to New York with an exemption, Maria Jolas has also fled to Manhattan taking your beloved grandson Claude. But you have survived a colostomy and pulmonary embolism, your caretakers: nurses, Marguerite (who has relinquished her son and gone to fight the war in her own way) and Lydia have survived months of your bullying, and so you remain. The doctors say you've been given four years to live. Since you actually died, and even when you came back and lingered you were not expected to live – the nurses call you *The Risen*.

You call it a second life, say you feel like a teenager again, that the pain wakes you up, hones your senses to a fine point of focus.

Lydia hires out-of-work actresses to model for you (no one else would accommodate your 3AM- 6AM morning work session), cleans your almost-empty studio (finished works in the bank for "the partition of assets," unnecessary furniture in storage, pets gone or fled), accompanies you on your noon walk, helps you travel to your visits with Bonnard in Le Cannet, and brings hot coffee and croissants when Bussy or Roualt visit your studio.

During your afternoon nap you review your life: confused young man, Fauvist, Rebel in Paris; adrift and at large in Manhattan, Los Angeles and on Fakarava; the Resussicated in Vence, Elder Statesman in Nice, *(soon to be National Treasure – as one of the lost French Artists of postwar France)*. You had planned to die, sent Pierre and George Duhuit letters, consulted with lawyers, drafted wills and bequests, last testaments, consigned your reputation to fate, made peace with your unfinished work. Now, unable perhaps to finish your work, but able to make considerable headway into what you had considered entirely lost to you, you renew your commitment to your painting as your only purpose.

Still Life with Magnolia, Fall 1941

Your style has changed. Will they notice? A young man will be ridiculed if he shows fear; an old man is only pitièd.

Every object on this table is bizarre, sea creature like, submerged in the carmine background, underwater. The scalloped mauve pitcher mimics the scalloped yellow and black-spotted nautilus shell, with its repeating Fibonacci spirals. The spiky, artichoke-colored magnolia leaves repeat the ridges of the shell. The cinabrese round mirror or plate behind the citrine vase shouts like a gong. The artichoke-green vase curves up into an oddly normal arabesque among all the fantastical, sea-creature shapes. Flanking each side of the mirror, the fat artichoke-green vase, and tiny slate gray vase with leaves are both monochromatic, with darker slate outlines and decorations. Because we are underwater, everything is flat; nothing casts its shadow. The cinabrese interior of the mirror reflects nothing but a dimmer view of the carmine background. So, these shapes do not exist? They are floating in water? In space? In the carmine-cinabrese mind of the viewer, of the painter, who has been given a second life? Or perhaps taken it? Snatched it away, like these objects have been snatched from their context? Is this what dying feels like? What being revived looks like? Is this what the world looks like after being reborn? It casts no shadow? You are submerged, underwater? Is death the only mirror that does not reflect? Where you cannot see yourself?

Interior with Bars of Sunlight, 1942

You see color differently now. The background is a pale grey-blue you rarely use, and the high, rectangular panels, red a brick red, almost cinnabar. The steps and floor that give a sensation of depth, pushing back into the room, are a mud brown alternating with ochre. Oddly, the signature stripe is black.

For the first time, we cannot see out the window. We see only its slightly darker blue shutters. The chaise's brick red stripes match the horizontal panels, and the stool matches the mud brown/ochre stairs and floor. The woman on the chaise is white, except for her ochre outlines and hair. She faces the window. We imagine she can see out – see what we cannot.

War is a terrible thing. Loss of your grandson Claude who, with his mother Marguerite's blessing, has been carried off by a stranger to New York City for safekeeping. Devastation. Artists and collectors rushing to hide their paintings and sculptures in underground vaults. Oncoming tanks and troops, rattle and stamp, rattle and stamp. Fleeing into the hills, away from the beloved and so necessary sea. Estrangement from your wife, the relinquishing of everything you once knew.

To Die Again, Winter 1942

Jean and Marguerite have left you to die again, or that's what the doctor says you'll do. Actually, they are nearby – Marguerite in Cannes, Jean in Antibes – they've left you alone so they may join the Resistance, and fight the War, each in her or his own way.

So, you refuse to die, refuse to leave the world before this horrible war is over. Eventually, when the trees drop their leaves, and in the parks the Bocce players put their sweaters on, your pains abate, you start eating again, defy the doctors.

Move to Villa le Reve, Vence, July 1943

Now that you and Lydia are up in the mountains, with the long view to the water, you take the long view yourself, considering yourself abandoned, forgotten, taken out to the garden compost pile like so many kitchen scraps. No one can think about anything but The War now. You can't blame them. There are so many artists now, so many demanding more and more attention. You have no wish to compete.

Because no dealers, collectors, sons or daughter will phone you, you don't need a telephone. Even your doves have flown away, looking for red ants' eggs.

Because there is nowhere to drive now, no exhibitions to stage, no canvases to frame, no deadlines, no opera impresarios yelling and raving at choreographers and composers, you don't need a car

Lydia keeps the studio clean. Except for a chest of drawers, the bed, a table, the easels and stools, you have put everything in storage. You take sheets of pure, saturated colors, then use the scissors to cut out their shapes. Visitors say the colors are blinding, even with the studio window shuttered. But they satisfy you like the glint off the sea, the silvery water – that sharpness, that edge. You want to become your blue, your morpho blue. The only blue that matters.

Jazz Cutouts, 1943

You begin to illustrate Mallarmé's *Poésies*, how do they become jazz? Color and line, why are they not the same thing? How are they fused? What unites them? Unifies them?

First they are flame throwers, carts and horses, circus of your childhood. Then they are mythical – Icarus, the falling, falling. Then they are the magical organic shapes of seaweed, pomegranates, birds, fish, the wavy philodendron leaves in the studio.

The scissors guide your hand, the color is lush and deep, nothing restrains you, no friction from the canvas or brush slows your quicksilver movements to make the shape. You carve out the shapes that haunt your memory, thinking this will exorcise them from your sleep, your waking visions. Tériade wants a book, you know you will write it yourself, in the chubby round script like arabesques, like your line drawings, to illustrate again what you've already shown in the solid colored shapes, where edge creates line. Cutting creates line. You are carving color. You are, for a moment, happy.

Marguerite Missing, 1944

What good are the celebrations in the north, people screaming and running through the streets of Montmartre and Montparnasse in Paris, dancing and slipping, arranging their hair, drinking from and jumping into fountains, breaking bottles on the cobblestone streets – what good if no one can find Marguerite? She is not still imprisoned by the Gestapo. Is the Resistance hiding her? If so, why can't Jean find her? He says they are not so organized, and even then, no one would know.

You want to hire a car and drive through the woods, from the high snowy mountains of the Alps west, west, west, until you arrive at the great marshlands and wild horses of the Camargue, taking in a giant swath of Provençal meadows, hills, fields, lavender, sunflowers, fortified hill towns, and countryside, until you locate her.

People whisper outside your doors, you can hear them, speculating, wondering if she could have survived six months of Gestapo interrogations. You will not hear of it. She is alive. You can feel her pulse in your own veins. She is your daughter, your oldest, you have nursed her through operations, her throat, sat by her bedside while she slept, and you know she is alive. She is not in a cellar somewhere – she is outside; but not under a blazing sun – you feel the dappled sunlight on her arm.

Marguerite Visits, January 1945

It is too horrific to even think of, your own daughter beaten with metal spikes and leather knotted strands. It's Medieval, the Inquisition. But six months later she visits, she sits down on the yellow divan and without your asking, she tells you about it. All the sickening smells, the damp, the dirt, the smeared blood. When she is finished talking, she sighs and looks around the room. You can see she was gone during the telling, but has come back to the room, and yourself, her father. It is so easy for her now, to leave and come back like this. It is what the artist always does. What takes its toll on artists.

Everyone says she is radiant, but really she is other worldly, you can see from her translucent whiteness of her skin, her glassy eyes, she has already passed over. Maybe when she gave up Claude to the safety of New York, maybe when she was near death, hiding in the woods, maybe before that when she slit her wrists.

Having survived all of this she appears triumphant to most, but to you – cadaverous. Ethereal, ghost-like. A shroud.

As the Maeghts' rattling *Deux Chevaux* drives away down the hill toward Nice, carrying your radiant daughter back to Paris, you watch reluctantly from the window. For days after, you sit and stare at your work, only half-hearing Lydia moving canvases, cleaning, gesso-ing.

Postwar Cimiez, 1946

Back in Cimiez, you are flying now with your doves. You do not even notice Lydia, the studio assistants, the plumber, the carpenter, the models, delivery boys, the visitors. In the garden beyond the window: olive, orange, palm.

Lydia tells you that all the visitors stare in awe at your faster than light movements with the scissors, hands flying like your doves, always coming back to you, to rest with you, after flight.

You follow the feeling of the line, and watch as the color gets brighter and brighter. Lydia tells you they say your studio is another world, a world apart, a world outside this postwar France, postwar Europe. You have made your mind real. It exists in the studio itself, in the cutouts on the walls, in the doves and philodendron, in the silvery wheelchair and your presence, become august, fingers flying, arms flapping like wings, wave of elbows like the sea swell crashing. You have made your mind manifest in everything around you.

Or so Lydia tells you. Down in the street afterwards, they stand for a while amazed, talk in small groups, gesticulate with their hands. As they go by with batons of baguettes, neighbors stare at these astounded talkers, gesticulators. Neighbors also lean from windows. They see a car – *Matisse is going out*, they say. They see a stranger – *Visitors are going in*, they say.

Aragon Visit, Vence, 1946

You think of him as the thin man, elegant and still. (Really, he is starving; they all are. It's despicable.) But back from Paris, he acts agitated, but the studio seems to calm him.

You draw quick sketches of him, while his breathing slows. He cannot stop moving though; he is thinking of Nice and Paris during the war, his mother just dead, chased by the Gestapo, he came to you then, and you drew tens of sketches of him, every feeling he'd had then, while Aragon watched, examining you, since he had been crafting an essay about you.

Now, like you, he seems to want to contain all those feelings, withdraw them. Who wouldn't?

No one should have endured what people lived during this war. Those who make it through, they never find their pre-war self. They never find safety, innocence again. Never relax into themselves again. In every shadow on the face, you see the ways in which they are haunted by the cruelty others have inflicted. Fires, shots, crashing buildings, the destruction of art, architecture. That is, in itself, something. But the cruelty, the reveling in another's suffering, once you've seen this, you never feel safe again.

You always feared something inside you, so afraid you were reluctant to sleep; because there, in sleep, you might come face to face with them. Now, you know what those fears are, but still, you do not welcome sleep; you would still rather run away.

You try to be gentle with him, this postwar Aragon; Lydia tries to feed him. It is difficult to eat when you have been starving for years. A whole nation, all of Europe, starving for years. The cavities of the face and collarbone, hollowed out, grayish. You draw his elegant jacket instead. For we are a country glamourous in the midst of suffering, we are artful and cunning. We practice a sophisticated treachery.

Aimé Maeght

Before the war ended, and Bonnard helped him open his Paris gallery, Maeght was a printer in Cannes, where he met your good friend Bonnard. When Maeght put a Bonnard litho from a concert poster in his shop window and it sold immediately, he asked Bonnard for more.

They sat and talked. The more they talked, sitting in the back room of the printing shop, the more Maeght learned about the artists alive in Paris and in the south of France. In the leanest times of the war, Maeght decided to fight his own resistance, ferrying bread and paint to Bonnard, and other artists along the coast, when no one else could reach them. Risking his life to keep Bonnard alive, he became like a son to the great painter, who needed a son to love, to teach, to mentor.

Although you and Bonnard were contemporaries, only two years apart in age, he seemed older to you; starting with the same colors, you became bold while his art came from a calmer tradition. The war had made him so ill, killed him really. He did not last much longer, afterward – only two years. Some people cannot stand cruelty. It makes them sick. It kills them. Bonnard was like that, tender inside, and his canvases showed that.

But before Bonnard died, before the war had ended, he took Maeght to Paris and helped Maeght buy his gallery in Paris; the first show was your own paintings. So, Bonnard helped his adopted son – son of his heart.

Nelck, 1944-50

When Lydia takes pity on the Dutch refugee and painting student Annalies Nelck, adopts her almost as a daughter, and puts her to work running errands and cleaning, you do not object. You know Lydia needs someone to care for and love, someone to bring up as her own. Here is someone to feed, calm, and love.

For yourself, you enjoy Nelck's awe at the bright white, the high ceilings of the studio, your imposing figure in bed, cutting pure color with scissors.

You always felt the voyeur, staring at your models with such intensity; now Nelck is the voyeur, watching Lydia position models, watching you draw. Your game is to draw her when she isn't looking – almost impossible – she looks constantly, at any movement of Lydia's elbow, at any shadow cast by the philodendron as the light shifts.

You teach her to draw the line, then a table; you teach her to paint a still life, then a figure; teach her color and line; find her modest buyers in trim suits, allow her to admire your skills and technique.

You see your young self in her – the person in awe of plants and the sea, in awe of blues, in awe of Renoir. She watches you and Lydia argue, as if searching for some secret essence of companionship. When she sees Lydia take your anger away with your tea tray, but leave you your defiance with the scissors and colored sheets, even share in it – she thinks perhaps she had found that essence.

Lettres Portugaises, October 1946

Vence: orange, olive, palm. Tériade wants more drawings: *Lettres Portugaises*.

You can't sleep at night. If you do, you relive the capture, torture, and flight stories Marguerite told you.

So how can you express such raw emotions? You, purveyor of reticence, hiding on a hill down, but not far from the sea. How can you?

Nelck your model – she follows Lydia around the studio; your eyes follow her, and your hands move quicksilver lines around the page. You don't look down, don't need to, just toss the page on the floor and move on to another. Single portrait, double, she does not realize she is chewing on the tips of her fingers. She is not surrounded by hunger, but enveloped by it. Subsumed in it. Her blouses hang on her, bereft, disconsolate. What has she seen? What has she lost? What do the sketches show?

Nelck, the name reminds you of a shellfish, or a deep sea creature. But the girl herself is more birdlike, edgy, cautious, ready to flee. Always taking a strand of her chestnut hair and moving it back, away from her face. Blue eyes staring. Tilting her head. She looks at you warily. When cornered, she chews her fingertips.

But you have many doves, so you know the ways and feelings of birds. One kind of bird, anyway. A homing bird. This is a migrating bird, in mid-flight across thousands of miles, stopping for a night in a foggy, dark place.

Models, Postwar Nice, 1946

Boredom seems to you to be the last option, after witnessing such breaking apart of families, cities, buildings, souls. Maybe they are just exhausted? In some deep, fragile detachment from what they lived through?

You ask her to position herself on the yellow divan in a draped attitude that suits her ennui. She complies, stares out the window. Nelck tells you these girls are society girls from Cannes, who can't find work or entertainment. You both wonder how Lydia finds them.

After a few minutes of dissonance, you realize you need another dress, and you can't find Lydia, so you go to her room. She is not there. You leaf through her closet, and still you do not find this dress, the cornflower blue one with the white ruffle from collar to hem. You notice a suitcase at the back of the closet, and think perhaps that is where she keeps the models' dresses. For a vain moment you think perhaps inside you will find the sketches you gave to Nelck – that Lydia has stored for safekeeping.

You open the suitcase. Instead of the cornflower dress, or your drawings for Nelck, you find the necessities of flight: a toothbrush and hairbrush, five pairs of underwear and two brassieres, comfortable walking shoes, three sturdy and nondescript dresses.

You shut and clasp the case, try to reposition it exactly where it was. You shudder because you have opened your future death. You see it in a flash: your daughter coming up in a rush from Nice, frightened models because Lydia had disappeared, you laid out on the bed in the corner of the studio, more peaceful than you ever were in life, your hands clasped across your belly.

You come back into the studio and tell the bored model she has the afternoon off. She laughs and lights a cigarette. You will draw doves and philodendron leaves for the rest of the afternoon. You will cut out one oak leaf in different shapes. You are the future – you're always telling Nelck your work isn't understood until 30-50 years after it's made – so you don't like to see a future in which only your body remains, and Lydia has fled.

Tahiti – Oceania 1946

For fifteen years you refused to speak of it. You refused to paint it. You lied to protect its treasure. You said that Oceania was boring, tedious in its beauty, its peace, its luxury of nature, all bird and sky. You said you needed the conflict of France.

But twenty years later the pressure of those images can no longer be contained. A seafoam sky with white birds. Seaweed. Strips of water with swimmers. They come out of you in cut outs, cut out of you. Excised. The most exotic octopi and sea creatures, squid, fish, elaborate seaweed in three colors.

No walls. No borders. And so you create a new beginning. Once again.

Oceania The Sky, Oceania The Sea, 1946

Philodendron Leaves become seaweed, become another cutout white and pale blue sky becomes Polynesian, fuchsia masks become Eskimo or Japanese, seafoam and teal dancers Creole, Tahiti rushes back like tide into memory, smell, damp sea sprays, in dreams, in cutouts of weeds like philodendron. Deliciously scalloped seaweed. So expressive in forms. So satisfyingly curved. So sensual. So much like reawakening to life.

Nothing so flat as looking straight up or straight down – flatness achieved, finally, by covering a stain on the wall, and letting that shape remain, adding, till Zika wants a silkscreen. And so it is, all the shapes, become the smells, the sounds, the light, Tahiti comes back, comes into the studio, but you are the only one who can feel the salty ocean froth come off the waves and hit your face.

Polynesia the Sky, 1946

So tan. Not the blue Tahiti. The blue Tahiti is its patchwork of sky-blue and indigo, its repetition of flailing bird wings, lolling seaweed, and jagged starfish like Icarus falling from the sky, underneath, the curious squid curls up, the froth lifts tentacles from the bottom border, the sides, and seaweed hangs down from the top border. Again, there is nothing flatter than looking down, down past the seabirds to the sea itself, and then down further, inside the water, where the filtered sunlight waves the water-lifted plants aloft. Blue and white. Anything blue. Everything blue. Anything white. Every blue background for any white shape.

A secret. Don't tell. Witness. How do you capture love and whimsy in a shape? Look. Don't speak. Inhale. The sea is here. You have been missing it. I know. But now it is here.

The Fall of Icarus – 1947 – Jazz Cut Outs

It always comes back to this, seeking that radiance, getting too close, and falling. This has become the rhythm of your life; you measure it this way, in these approaches to radiance and the subsequent falling back, like tides, like waves coming to shore and receding, like the sun rising and setting, like lives coming to their zenith and slowly declining. We are made from star dust*. You knew this: here he is: white, his heart a red star, the others he's falling through – yellow. The sky he's falling through – blue. Your signature black stripe behind him, like a chute in the sky. A shaman tunnel through the sky, within which Icarus descends back to earth. Or a shaft of darkness, instead of sunlight. A stripe of night sky. Shaft, chute, tunnel.

His edges are sharp like the stars, and his fall is lost hope, despair, regret, nostalgia. Foolishness is what he feels, foolishness to dream. And yet we dream.

Longing is the artist's reason to keep pushing forward. Everyone says so. So we fuel our longing. When does longing become regret?

The stars come from everywhere and so far away. There are so many, and yet Icarus is lonely, falling among them. His heart is like them, a star, and yet, surrounded by stars, he is lonely.

When the starlight finds us, from so far away, so much time has passed. It is no longer the same star first that sent its light out over the distance.

Distances we can't imagine, nor speeds – hurtling through space. Faster than time, and yet not outrunning it. How can that be? It's yet another paradox. The stars are beyond the reach of our longing. Infinite.

And yet, they are right next to Icarus. Can he reach out to them? And when he grabs them to arrest his fall, do they pierce his hand, burn it?

The reaches of space are unfathomable, and yet we send our deepest hopes into them. Heat, energy, light, movement – and yet no life.

If you were alone with the stars, what would they say to you? Would they speak orange? Would they be kind yellow? White hot? Would they smile mauve?

And if they spoke Cyrillic to you, would you answer back in a Tamil dialect? One of fifteen spoken?

Would your Brahmin heart speak to them of love, of desire, of the reds and oranges you see behind your eyes in the sunlight? Of longing and despair? *For I too can fly,* you tell them. *I can laugh. I can tell stories about my downfall. I can deflect the pain.*

White Algae on Red and Green, 1947

You see depth where there is only flatness. Like looking into the ocean.

Layers of color. White is a color. Lead white. Lime white.

The red of the algae is a brick red, lead red, not the bright flaming red of a cochenille beetle's shell ground to powder. Diamonds of red run down the algae's middle stem like vertebrae, like a spine. Your signature white stripe is green, a middle, grass green, center, background. The fronds are similar, except for the one on the middle right, that veers off and splits in two, then the lower half hangs limp, like a disappointment. The other fronds are moving, dancing, happy, quizzical, bemused. The image could be a six-legged salamander, climbing a wall.

No context: just the one leaf of algae, the one stripe of background. Isolated. Condensed. Synthesized. If you could reduce your Tahiti to one image, would it be this algae leaf? No: it wouldn't. You preserve essence in line, in purity of color, not in the number of objects. You would say there are many components to this cut-out, not just one algae leaf.

Claude: teenager, 1947

A teenager now, Claude wears blue jeans. He is a cool James Dean, a decade before the movie star, a decade before the invention of American teenagers. He is New York City's postwar swagger, art-world dominance, but yet – still the kind, adorable, loving grandson Claude. Yours to hold. Yours to love.

Visits are too short. As much as the skyline and buzz of New York enthrall you, you cannot live there, and his mother will not allow Claude to live here in the countryside or on the coast with you, as much as you'd like him to.

The remaining doves remember him; they love him too. They perch on his shoulders and peck his ears. His hair is soft, sand colored. His eyes a sharp blue, but not your blue. He smiles. He smiles at you. He loves you.

He sits as close as he can, and watches you work. He asks about the colors. When he looks around the room, at the Tahiti cutouts, he says he feels underwater, and oddly, he likes that. You joke he has a future as a pearl diver, but he counters with the more masculine oceanographer, or scuba diver.

Claude always liked shiny glints of light off the dove cages, off the windows and the sea, so you think, while he describes to you all the modern shiny equipment, maybe this is more than a dream.

Since you don't know if this visit will be his last, you don't want him to go.

April 1947, back in Vence,

the war is truly over. Like the insomniac deprived of dream sleep, when allowed to sleep again – making up all the dreams he was deprived of – now, this spring, you paint all the canvases you would have the last three years, if the butcherous ending and aftermath of war had not kept you away from them.

You paint the table with a bowl of oranges and lemons, the window beyond; Nelck at the table in a cornflower blue shirt, the palm tree dominating the window, overpowering the vase of yellow and pink tulips on the table, carmine background and cinabrese wall surrounding the blue; Nelck in the Roumanian blouse, her hands primly intertwined on the now mauve table, elbows soft, forearms resting, the giant green pitcher (matching the high chair supporting her back) filled with white wildflowers, dahlias, mauve primroses even. The smaller vase clear, with grayish water and a few green and mud colored twigs.

You paint the raucous zigzagging background, bright fresh-blood red, with black Zs, a royal blue table strewn with more red apples and a vase over-toppling with green leaves, the window showing green with more black zigzags, and an orange splotch, that mirrors the orange circle on the wall with Nelck's face inside, the one orange shutter.

You paint the window again, with something massive, hanging purple from the indigo tree trunk outside, the wallpaper indigo and gray stripes, the woman at the table in citrine dress, the other blending into the indigo wall, as does the table, with its book and another clear vase, with bigger fronts of over-toppling leaves.

Then a calmer, black walled painting, with a serene tree in greens and yellows, serene gray readers at the grayish table, everything inside black or gray.

You continue like this, each painting different (except they are all flat), each painting more bizarre, or more calm. The nights, exhausted, you manage to sleep, but only for three hours, and then you start again.

Illustrations for *Les Fleurs du mal* de Baudelaire, *Florileges de l'amours de* Ronsard, *Poemes de Charles* d'Orleans, 1947-50

Artists feed themselves on longing; everyone says so. Why not, therefore, express your longing, not in your paintings – which take days, weeks or months to execute – but in your line drawings, quicksilver creations, celebrating the curves and beauty of women's bodies.

The models move at will, they turn on the divan, they nap, they go to the window. Your eyes follow them; your intensity making them uneasy.

The drawings are executed so quickly, on a knife edge, then sail, zigzagging to the wooden floor. They scatter there, where you can glance at them, reassured.

Other times you draw from memory – the scenes of myth or story that match the poem you are commissioned to illustrate. It might be a face edged like a leaf, bodies entwined, two huddled doves, a lute or lyre rimmed with laurel leaves, a woman's back, or her face resting in her arm, asleep.

Your family insists you must not show or sell these drawings, but then of course you must. They are well received in London, over the protests of journalists, critics, Amélie, Marguerite.

When the fine papered editions of poems come out, the drawings work in tandem with the poems, as equals, side by side. They are not really illustrations, though you allow others to call them that. They are mutually enhancing art forms, tied together, like music and movement in dance, or dance and music in ballet.

Interior with Dog: Etta Cone dies, 1949

The second sister is dead now, and your paintings on their way to the Baltimore Museum, as she bequeathed in her will. You were always fonder of the second sister, the gentler, more timid, more uncertain sister. It would have been considered natural, since you spent more time with her, but you wouldn't admit this to anyone. You felt her indecision as your own; you felt her cowardice as your own. You knew how much more difficult it was for her to climb out of fear and into ownership of her own life, because you had done it yourself, at such a great cost: the steep cost of losing a marriage, losing the respect of children, enduring oppressive scrutiny, derisive ridicule.

What are sisters, anyway? Pierre and Jean have their sister. You did that. Your wife Amélie has a sister, whom she relies on, when she is desperate or near nervous collapse. She recovers from that, and goes to fight a war you try to shun. Both sisters in your family, Amélie and Marguerite, fought the war while you painted. You shudder when you think of it.

Etta. You called her submissive. Attentive. Less beautiful. To have a sister means to always be compared to her. When she asked you to paint her dead sister's portrait, she was reminded that those comparisons last beyond death, last forever.

Etta outlasted her sister for twenty years. Claribel, the pathologist. The president of the women's medical college. Etta the musician. Gertrude, the object of her longings, introduced her to Picasso first, in 1905, and you a year later; Leo taught her how to collect art. You are not compared to any brothers; but instead to Picasso, your nemesis, whom you call your younger brother. Etta came to you directly to buy paintings, not to the shows or galleries. You gave her and her sister some of your most important works, the *Blue Nude, Purple Robe with Anemones*.

Inventive, musical, various, Etta did not stop at paintings; she even bought the copper plates for your Mallarmé illustrations. She bought the painters before you and after you. Unlike Shchukin, wars and revolutions did not drive her away. She did not snub you on the streets of Nice.

Some of your models must have sisters. But these postwar models are bored, not shy. They are not mourning lost loves, lost brothers and sisters, like Etta. These models, so full of ennui, they know everything is within their reach. What happens when you can envision what you want so clearly, the love you want, the person you want, the life you want, but it is entirely out of reach?

You even gave her one of your favorite paintings, *Interior with Dog*.

Do Not Judge Your Art by The Amount of Work You Put Into It

You are always talking about your mistakes. Your biggest, you say, is that you let yourself believe the amount of hard work, frustration, energy you put into a painting made it more valuable. The more frustration, the greater the work. As you look back now, (despite my attempts to warn you not to), you see that this is not the case: many of your best works came willingly, in a sudden fusion of understanding, sympathy, and care. Pinpoint accuracy. Your cutouts come this way now. You are working on raw nerve and past insight.

You will not let others learn from your mistake, though. Better that they feel they must work hard every day. The daily life of a painter, grinding colors, stretching canvasses, drawing, choosing colors, applying brushstrokes, changing brushstroke styles, layering a composition, balancing, blotting out and trying again. All artists must have this daily habit, you insist, and if the sudden fusion of understanding produces a work, that is a blessing. It is no less valuable than the hard won works. They are all hard won. They are all a product of this daily hard work.

When I tell you that you are rambling now, contradicting yourself, you pat me on the head and go on with your work, as you say you must. Your saturated colors are blinding to others, though moderately bright to you. Your brain has adjusted to the intensity, absorbed it, like the sun, taking back is flares. You live in your own magical world now, of doves, bright colors, shapes, the view from window, the giant and tall high-ceilinged room; a magical world people feel the moment they enter the studio. It feels much like being blessed, or entering a Moroccan garden, or visiting sacred land.

No Walls, No Boundaries

Time is malleable. We feel it going faster and slower, looping back on itself, stumbling, bubbling, even laughing. A scientist says that the pyramids draw so much gravity time slows down around them.

So why can't space be malleable? Not all spaces have equal qualities. Some are magical: walking through the woods, you suddenly come to a wide open meadow, with fog up to your knees. Across the meadow, a twelve-point buck stands, staring at you, refusing to budge. You are enchanted by the magic of the space, as if you'd stepped into a different world entirely.

Now you want art without borders, without walls, without limits of space or time. Something hangs in the air, but is not suspended; something lies flat, but has no borders; something cannot be contained. You want to change the nature of space, or discover its secrets, but to create, not destroy.

We all long to escape space, but we believe we can do so only when we die. You want to make art in that space, that in-between space – a living art.

And why shouldn't you? Why shouldn't you be the one to make quantum art? Quark art? Neutrino art? Why can't it be you? Why can't time and space shift? Adjust? Why not in a painting? Why not in your paintings?

Like the caves at Lascaux, we must all go back and look again at your paintings. How do they make us feel? What do they make us know? Experience? What do they speak to us?

The Liberation of Vence, August 27, 1945

When you thought it was over, the bombs started like a train come off its tracks. Afraid of being inside, you, Lydia and Nelck huddled in the garden with the oranges, palms and olive trees. At least you could see stars. Nelck had come out clutching a thick book to her chest. Lydia pried it from her fingers. Bergson. You had never thought about duration before, a moment gone before you have had time to measure it. Intuition, that you knew. Introspection, imagination, that too, you had experimented with, like a scientist, your entire life.

Lydia thought you'd gone mad, when at certain moments in the book you would break out laughing. Nelck would look over at her, blinking her eyes rapidly, perhaps in despair. Lydia thought this was not time to lose your heads, and said so. But you were busy listening to Nelck read Bergson saying you *should go on creating, endlessly*, such as what you did. You laughed because, well, because you had no idea he knew you so intimately.

When Nelck read that intuition can only be found in the absolute, you laid down in the moss and looked up at the stars. You could hear the shells explode, but they were far enough across town that they did not make you jump.

Every few hours, Nelck would put the book down in the moss, rush into the house, her apron flapping, come back with water and bread.

You tried to stop laughing. While you traced the line of the palm fronds with your eye, Nelck was reading something about imagination and perception. When dawn came, Nelck and Lydia were exhausted, but you felt refreshed, and went right back to work, while they took a short walk to see how close the shelling had come to the Villa le Reve. In Paris you survived a snowy winter without enough coal, you've survived exhaustion and a ferocious reaction to penicillin, now this.

Villa the dream. When you first moved in you thought it should be a villa of dreams, not of dream, but having lived here on and off, for several years now, and having almost died here, you agree that the villa is more about the idea of a dream than any concrete dreams. But you must get back to the concrete dreams, so you pick up the scissors, and pull a saturated color sheet off the wall. Sculpting color is what you do now. It's a new way of painting and you've created it.

Laughter needs an echo.

Picasso and Gilot Visit, 1947

You ride horseback, take walks, visit each other's studios, exchange paintings, try on each other's style. He leads a group; you work alone. When the group's facile Cubism eclipses the more complex and profound quests you are pursuing alone, you criticize his popularity, his facile line; but because he is your friend, no one else is allowed to do it. Stein favors him. She ridicules you with eggs: only scrambled for Matisse. When the critics pair you, when the galleries combine your shows, you think it the most farfetched duo imaginable. But after the second War, when the art market flees to your son Pierre's precious Manhattan, with his electric skyline, the French museums start to buy your work, MOMA is creating a gallery for the both of you.

And so, the rivalry cools, and your younger brother, as you secretly think of him, whom you secretly admire, begins to visit again, urged by his forty-years-younger partner Françoise Gilot. They come when Françoise is pregnant with their child Claude, named just like your beloved grandson.

He smiles, jokes, fawns, finally loses his temper at you. Françoise appears sympathetic and confused. She's only known Picasso four years, and has never seen him try to please anyone, or become so frustrated in an attempt.

They come to you in Vence at the Villa le Reve. The light through the window hits his shoulder. Hit. Françoise, a painter herself, admires the space, steps up close to the cut-outs on the wall. While Picasso rages about your mutual friend, the publisher Tériade, you sit quietly, smile, fold your hands on your basin of lap. You think about how soon he will know old age. How never will he openly acknowledge your friendship.

Lydia brings tea. The women, struggling painter and struggling medicine student turned studio assistant, exchange glances. Picasso laughs and laughs. Suddenly you know there will be more visits like this. Though he will never visit enough to suit you.

Chapel of the Rosary at Vence, 1948-51

You put your blue in it, the only blue, but that's a secret. And it will remain so for a very long time. You put the blue of the sky and some water, in special places, the green of the plants, and the lemon yellow of the sun. Nothing else matters, and because that is so, you turn everything else bone white: the tiles, the walls, or the palest shade of wood you can find, the beechiest beech-tree color, sand colored wood.

You defile the church, the chapel, the white tiles. You paint crude images in lead black on the bone-white tiles. Stations of the cross. An angry response to the elegance of the beautiful blue/yellow/green windows, and the, sleek mantle, bronze crucifix, bronze candleholders, candle snuffs; priest's vestments: chasuble, maniple, stole; covering of the chalice, benches – in sum, all the paraphernalia of Catholic ritual.

The gossip begins. The nun is young and beautiful. The work is intense and spiritual. Spirit made flesh. No one believes in purity of belief, of color, or of flesh. No one believes in chaste intensity.

Picasso complains: *Why a chapel?* Catholics complain: *Why the crude drawings of the stations, of the violence, of the redemption.*

Everyone steps in to object, to slow your work, as if churches have never been decorated by artists! What of Michelangelo's Sistine Chapel ceiling? What of da Vinci's Last Supper? What of Gozzoli's Siennese frescoes?

But you are too old to slow down now. The slender candlesticks shine. They are Matisse. The narrow blond-wood podium gleams. It is Matisse.

The priests' robes resemble Japanese kimonos, as reinterpreted by Matisse (reminiscent of the Song of the Nightingale costumes), or a Mongolian Shaman's wrap – hidden under his fringe. But there is no fringe.

Peeking out through the tall, tree trunk-like narrow stained glass, the purest royal blue (perhaps the one you've searched for all your life), the purest lemon yellow, the purest grass green. There is redemption here, in this simplicity, in this fervor. See how the light slants through? Isn't god in that light? See how the white tiles shine? Isn't god in that gleam? See how everything fits together, like a painting? How all the lines and proportions mesh, dovetail, into a perfect work of art? Isn't god in the perfection of those proportions?

Relationships

Most artists say their focus is on movement. For you, if we take you at your word, it is about relationships: Artist to model, objects to each other on the picture plane.

Also consider: the relationship of inside to outside, flatness to depth, twos to threes, oranges to lemons, lemons to goldfish, goldfish to bowl, bowl to table, table to chair; self-portrait to studio portrait, line to curve, curve to volume, color to form, color to line; and most important, perfection of line to perfection of color.

Extrapolate to other relationships: first, your painter self to your other selves: yourself as father to yourself as painter, husband to painter, fauve painter to painter of arabesque, painter to draughtsman.

But also others to you: colleague to painter, friend to painter, rival painter to painter, and so on, the painter to: assistant, landlord, shopkeeper, greengrocer.

We don't think of these things, because if we do, the mind begins to spin.

Blue Nudes, Cutouts, 1952

Blue. *Bleu Nu.* Again. The color. The only color really. Sky and sea. Sea in certain special places. Places where indigo mixes with aquamarine. Seas like that. Tahiti, Bora Bora, Santorini, Nice.

You pretend that all the colors matter, but only this matters, this one blue. The blue you never see. The blue in between the indigo and aquamarine, the blue that is neither royal, nor cornflower, nor turquoise. Not Egyptian, nor cerulean, nor lapis lazuli, nor malachite. A pure blue. The purest blue you have ever seen.

You found it as a child, lost it; now you find it again. This is how you know your life is ending, in the same way when, as a child, you knew your life was beginning.

The arabesque has become a spiral, the spiral a circle, the circle your life – the end moving closer and closer, back to the beginning point.

Now, to fuse pure color, pure line, and a woman's body; seated, standing; near, distant; only the curved shape that embodies straight lines within it. So mysterious, but so familiar. A slight tilt of head or arm. A slight raise of thigh or foot. Angle of the head. Lever of the elbow. Zest of the foot. Pique of the nose. Enigma in the corner of the eye.

A Space Where Things Can Happen Differently

A canvas is that space. Tahiti, on the bottom half of the world, the other hemisphere, is that space.

Things happen differently in the southern hemisphere. Winter is summer. Summer is winter. The light is more ethereal, luminescent, pearl-tinted, perhaps hinting at the pearls in the lagoon. The space feels more voluminous. The plant leaves are bigger – huge, even. Spiritual is sensual. Sensual is spiritual. Space is boundless.

The people are beautiful, with their rounder features and coppery chocolate skin. They are kinder. They should forgive you nothing, you, a representative of the colonizers. But they welcome you. Pauline, only twenty-six years old, meets you at the boat, even though she hasn't received your letters. Commandeering her boyfriend Ernest and his Buick, driving you to the new hotel, *The Stuart*, no phones, no doors, who needs privacy? Who needs muffled conversations, requests that no one else can here? You do. Your sense of modesty demands it.

And all the blues – the inkiest blue of the Pacific, almost black, turning the sky a chalky grey; the teal and slate blue fishes in the market.

So is this the other space, unreal to you at least (very real to them). You now seem unreal, pale and sickly like some deep sea creature deprived of light. Is this a place where things can happen differently? To you, at least? Not yet. Not until Fakarava.

In four days on Fakarava, you become certain of what you suspected all along: that all life is sensual, not just young women. The vanilla plant, the intensity of the sun on your face and shoulders, the lagoon's edge, the underwater ripple, the bright coral, the striped fish – all sensual. And more, perhaps more important, all this sensuality is spiritual: that which contains life, beauty, contains meaning.

You guard this secret closely for thirty years, while Pauline sends you packages with deep, rich vanilla pods, dried banana, pandanus woven into swatches, and you draw the enormous breadfruit leaves that look like your philodendron, apples become your pomegranates. stars your spiky, starfish-shaped yellows.

All the Fakarava terns, albatross, become your doves; all the Fakarava parrot fish, shark, grouper become your goldfish, its clams and crabs your conches, taro and coconut becomes pomegranate. But what are they, really? Distilled essences, incorporated logos of your experiences on Fakarava. For you, all birds are doves, all fruits are pomegranates, all plants are philodendron, all stars are yellow spiky starfish, all colors are your only blue.

For you are finally underwater here, immersed in your blue, with bright yellow and pink tufts of coral, and azure and vermillion-striped fish as your guideposts, the surface of the water above like a windowpane.

And all peace, all enlightenment, all contentment, all delight is Fakarava.

Color

Go out into the sunlight and shut your eyes? What do you see? Bright pinks and oranges, a brilliant red. A deep purple and burgundy. Colors so intense and bright you never see them anywhere else except inside your eyelids when you stand in the sun – or in your Matisse paintings. That is the only other place you see them.

Where did you first see them? The Giottos in Padua? in Vermeer?

Cezanne

Cezanne was everyone's master, and yet, you all branched out from him in a different way. You all selected one or two things to explore. Some saw volume and became Cubist. Some saw color and became what a critic called Fauves. You passed through the Fauves, but sought both intensity of color and an arabesque line. You became Matisse.

Pauline Sends Vanilla

When the package comes, you set it carefully on the work bench. It is a small, rectangular box, wrapped in brown shipping paper. The stamps show bright orange coconut crabs and lime green palm trees. Throughout the day, you watched as the sunlight cast shadows on it. Your assistants, whispered to each other, and trying not to look at it, pretending it wasn't there.

At the end of the day when the assistants have left to shop for dresses, and Lydia is making tea, you stand over the package, resting the palm of your hand on it. Outside, leaves are rustling, but they are nothing like the palms whipping in the wind at Fakarava.

The package wrapping is neatly folded and sealed. Inside, the wooden box's contents are packed in shredded coconut threads from the inside of the shell, and each item is wrapped in a banana leaf. Pauline has sent you a package of vanilla beans, dark, almost espresso colored, shiny and iridescent, like the lagoon. She has sent you news clippings about a murder on Bora Bora, and a tapa cloth with repeating triangular designs etched into it.

You stretch the tapa cloth over the divan, then step back to look at it. Before tapa, you never thought tree bark would be cloth.

Tériade's Villa Natacha, 1953

It starts with the plane tree sketches in 1941: *I'll imitate the Chinese*, you tell Aragon, I'll distill the form to its essence. You make upwards of thirty sketches then, some you highlight with white gouache – all of a single plane tree, with its balanced branches, alternating out – right and left – from the thick trunk.

But your friendship with Tériade has started long before this, in '29: with your cutouts on the cover of his magazine Verve, illustrating poetry books for him, then most recently your own book of cutouts, Jazz. Afternoons in the garden of the Villa Natacha, other artists and publishers met there too, and in the convivial Greek way, a great feast was laid in the dining room, where everyone drank and sang, until Tériade began to throw plates, and jump up on the table, intimidating all those who were not from his sun-washed islands. They had the Greek light in them, the glare. Here it was much calmer, more sedate.

When he shows you the corner of that dining room for your sketch, you immediately think of the plane tree, and when he mentions the window that needs your stained glass, you think of your Chinese fish, distilled, down to its slippery, leaf-green essence.

So, you work, on borrowed time (for you expected to die five years earlier, and the doctors expected you to die a decade earlier), and you make these gifts for Tériade, your great friend, but more importantly, your collaborator.

On white-glazed ceramic tiles, you draw a tree in the corner of his dining room, three branches with alternating leaves, spanning on one wall, out over his seat at the table, facing the doorway; then the other side of the tree, three matching branches with alternating leaves, spanning out on that wall, on your side of the table, facing the window. Together now, sheltered and embraced by the tree along two walls, you sit in rattan chairs at a blonde table, where you eat his Greek okra stew, his chicken with lemons, looking out over the wide expanse of lawn cypress and palm trees and below, the shimmery bay.

Your window is installed at his Villa Natacha, with its round stained glass violas, and above, the row of three Xs, like a game of chance or a love message, or both. Below these, your fish, iconic philodendron shape, and seaweed, bordered on either side with vermillion violas. A carmine boomerang shape holds up the rest, mirroring, the red stripe at the top.

Your plane tree keeps its simplicity, reaching out in black from the white tiled corner, and extended along both walls, like Tériade's welcoming arms. The Chinese fish sits snugly in the bottom of the window, topped by your signature philodendron leaf, and surrounded by orange violas.

The villa is small, and crowded with people, but the gardens are glorious and open. You often sit there, quietly, while your friend roams his property, roaring his Greek lion's roar. The arts are coming back to the south of France, postwar, the artists like you and Picasso, Chagall, have replaced the sorrowful losses of Renoir and Bonnard. Tériade and that Swiss, Skira, establish themselves as publishers and purveyors of the artists. Collectors like Maeght bring Braque, Miro, Giacometti. Tériade's warmth, the presence of the others like them, and the glinty light, bring these new artists into his orbit; unaccustomed to his brotherly warmth, they so want to be near him. The world of southwestern Europe, shut so tight during the war, is beginning to open up again.

He has interviewed you many times for his artists' series, and you have contributed much to his magazine *Verve*. But the most important thing you tell him, you tell him lastly:

"So liberty is really the impossibility of following the path which everyone usually takes and following the one your talents make you take."

You have less than a year to live.

Sadness of the King/La Tristesse du Roi, 1953

Of course, the king is sad. Why wouldn't you be? You are not looking at the shimmering horizon, the beautiful coastline, the zesty Mediterranean life, tart as a shiny lemon rind. You are in bed, or in the infernal metal contraption called a wheelchair, cutting out pure color into pure shape, and fixing those shapes together into pure harmony.

So beautiful: the deep blue in the upper left corner, balancing the grass green in the bottom right. The fuchsia middle drags the eye across the frame, left to right, and up, just a little. The green figure, sitting cross-legged in harem pants on steps of fuchsia and deep blue, with her hands raised in supplication, is poignant. Just out of reach, the ochre guitar, surrounded in a black oval decorated in moss-green flowers, a matching moss-green head, white hands that seem to play it, but do not touch. From waist up, a background of the deepest Egyptian blue. Somewhere between cerulean and malachite.

The guitar-king plays a song so sweet that yellow leaves dance around him. But no matter what the black-robed king plays, he is not consoled. How can a king console himself? There are troubadours for that. Musicians, dancers, court jesters. No matter. Never mind.

And the white on the left, with black circles and curves. Another guitar? Another figure? A ghost? Death?

A dancer perhaps, her gray-blue arms raised, the black swirls a robe swirling round, the prominent black dots – her nipples? The black feet. Or is death a woman in a white robe, with black head, nipples and feet?

Or, are these parts of the black-robed king, just out of reach? Beyond it the signature stripe of green, with yellow and orange leaves lifting up from its spiky leaf-base.

And what of the orange ball in the green, seated-figure's lap? Is the orange ball a drum? A tambourine? Is it the life the king would like to have back, to live again? Is it youth? Desire?

The king has worked so hard. Achieved so much. Are all endings sad, despite the fond memories, the love given and received? Are there, in the end, only questions?

And yet, we are believing the title, not the cut-out, the composition, the picture itself. The cut out looks and feels happy. The colors saturate happy. The flying leaves, surrounding everyone, swirl happy. The three together, guitar player, drummer, dancer, mix happy. The guitar player surrounded by dancer and drummer, berobed in flowers, beribboned by slats of saturated color, bespeckled with leaves, strums happy. The fuchsia, the chartreuse, the deep blue, the orange, the greens, the yellow: all resonate happy. The black head, nipples and feet, the black robe, tingle happy.

The Sheaf, 1953

To be sent to a collector on the intermediate shore: the eastern edge of the Pacific Ocean. To Los Angeles. One home of the 1950s Architectural Modernism. To Holmby Hills. To a very large, very spare, very white, ultra-modern house – a house like an unpainted canvas. And there, amongst the very white, very rectangular furniture, they will need a splash of color. A modern splash.

So, you build them just that: a modern splash. It comes up, giant, from the depths of your memory, Tahiti, a fan, a great multicolored wave, made from fronds of seaweed. Each piece a bright basic color: royal blue, brick red, light and dark orange, or grass green; and at the tip, some deep blacks emerge, to signal the end, the fringes, the never more.

There are three-frond algaes like a bird claw, four like a paw, five like a hand, eight like caterpillars, nine even. And in the middle, on the left, there is one, only one, fifteen fronds, in a grass green.

Some are small and light. Others are big and boldly colored, saturated with color. Like a splash. Like fireworks. To light up the big white rectangle. To satisfy the collector. To complete a commission. To keep your word.

Everyone is satisfied. The ceramic paneled mural occupies an entire wall on the enclosed patio, above a white rectangular sofa. White chairs and lamps look on from the sides. Dappled sunlight filters through, a dappling that mimics the mural, and reminds you of the filtered sun through the oaks, long ago, in your garden in Issy.

You have three months to live.

The Parakeet and the Mermaid, 1954

Between you, on the far left, the blue parakeet: slim, tail dropped down straight below an invisible perch, like a teardrop, and on the far right the arabesque blue Mermaid – back arched, fins tucked, arms above her head – lies a vast expanse of orange and green or purple coral, seaweed, algae, plucked or fallen royal blue pomegranates from one of the trees outside your studio (pomegranates that look suspiciously like apples), cut out from gouache in the mid-range, the simplest colors.

So, who or what is this mermaid? Is she the life you once had, when you were a vibrant young man? Is it your loves, one love in particular? Love in general? A woman? Women in general? Love of life? Zest? Zest for life?

Does it really matter? No. What matters is there are three panels of coral and seaweed between you, and a panel of same after her, but there is none behind you. You are perched, as if caged, as if at a window, looking directly at her, long and a slightly upward through your whole life. Throughout your own life. Might she be your aspirations, still out of reach? Might you still be looking forward, to what you strived for, not behind you, at where you wish most to return.

The mermaid is encircled by pomegranates, and flanked by two orange fronds of seaweed, pointing up. You are encircled by seaweed pointing down. The downward sadness of life spent? The up-reaching happiness of life lived? There are a few pomegranates near you, a few huddled below. One could almost make trails of pomegranates, like steps, and track them across the picture. Like a bird's hieroglyphic claw prints.

Little parakeet. Life lives on in your work. That is no consolation. Trapped in your wheelchair-cage, you want to be the life of the mermaid. You want to dive, swim, toss pomegranates, eat them, swirl, nap on seaweed as it floats on the surface, live the life of joy and excitement, pleasure and terror, you are destined to live. You want to start over. *Let me start again*, you whisper. *I am coming to you. We will start again.*

Always Goodbye

As life accumulates, you notice layers upon layers of goodbyes are piling up thick, like paint. At first you didn't notice it. But there were always goodbyes: to parents, the study of law, at first, then sometimes to studios (ten Quai St. Michel in Paris, the villa with its dappled gardens at Issy, Villa le Reve in Vence, One Charles Felix in Nice); to studio props like stools, easels, fabrics, sofas – not so difficult.

But then the paint thickens: saying goodbye sometimes to friends, more and more often to Paris; then you must say goodbye to models you've worked so intensely with, made discoveries with, gone deeper into painting alongside of – Lorette, Antoinette, their costumes their jewelry, their little pointy shoes; sometimes it is masters like Renoir who befriended you, believed when you did not, confirmed that what you felt was your only choice was indeed the exact right one.

You must say goodbye to masters of distraction: Diaghilev, Massine, Prokofiev; You must say goodbye to operas and ballets, props and sets, costumes and ballerinas, even. Moving paintings, created at such cost to your own.

And of course, there are the cats and dogs to say goodbye to, parrots and doves, violins and pianos. Issy. Eventually, the beleaguered wife, the estranged daughter, the aloof younger son and adoring older son.

Places. Some are easy to say goodbye to: the gray-blue dust of despair in Morocco. Then less so: retreat back into Normandy textile-town childhood and recuperation of Estretat. Then less still: obligations and sanctity of family in Issy.

Some are more difficult, especially if you changed there, if consciousness broke through to another place, if the rain-washed light is revelation, if its quicksilver washes you, and its brilliance illuminates the hidden parts of your instincts: Collioure, Vence. Nice. Then you entrench. You do not let go. You become: *The Hermit of the Avenue des Promenades. The Recluse of One Charles Felix in old Nice.*

You thought you could be alone, that you wanted it. Free of obligation. You want to paint alone, but of course you cannot. You need suppliers, assistants, you need models, you need dealers, buyers, collectors, gallery owners, museum administrators. You've created obligations to your own family, obligations of long standing.

Finally, there are the goodbyes of aging: saying goodbye to health, to mobility, to illusions, to hopes. Now you are both less alone and more alone than ever, simultaneously. They know your work more, but understand it less. After fifty years beyond it, they want you to remain a Fauve, a colorist. They want you to stay out of the chapel, away from nuns; out of Nice, away from Delektorskaya.

They want you to stay with your family, or stay a Fauve, or stay in Paris, become a has-been; but you refuse; you keep moving. Despite immobility, you move closer and closer to what you've been seeking all along: fusing pure color with pure line.

Always a Window: Observed and Observer

Not just in the studio, but also in the world. Mostly, the window looks out on the boats in the bay of Nice, their masts akimbo, sometimes the sky is gray with a white stripe and below, aquamarine water; sometimes the sky is lavender with apricot water.

Or the window is Vence, villa of dream – a large tree, beautiful curving branches, and an arabesque blotch of slate against a grayish, powdery blue sky.

Or the couple argues, and below you can see not only the tree whose leaves now cover its curvy branches, because you are facing straight on now, but the winding purple walk below.

Or the window faces a giant palm, and all you can see are palm leaves, fanning out in a navy and citrine kaleidoscope. Who knows what is beyond?

Or the window opens to a vast view of a bay, and a vast sky of indigo with pink bulges of clouds, stacked up against each other all along to the zenith.

Or the window beyond the cat with its paw in the fishbowl. The view a meadow, with lead white puffy tree leaves, a vermillion hill and azure sky. A view so deceptively simple as to be confused with a child's drawing.

Or mostly window, the Avenue des Promenades, the wide expanse of bay, little white bands of froth in the sea, little white sailboats navigating in and out of the froth under a cobalt-violet sky, with two tiny palm trees adorning the walkway, where tiny people seem to walk, observing and observed.

Or a green land, with a verdigris cliff, a malachite bay, and rust ochre sailboats beached and side-fallen on tawny and sienna strips of sand, approached by white frothy waves propelled by a violet-grey sea, all seen through grass-green shutters.

But outside demands inside to complete it, like sides of a coin. Can you have a body with no inside? Maybe for a landscape or a universe, but not for a body or a room.

So, inside from blue sky masts akimbo is a girl asleep in an aquamarine blue bed in a turquoise blue room. Her celestial blue sheets match the celestial blue ceiling.

Inside from the apricot masts akimbo is a fuchsia striped tablecloth, on which a green platter is laid, strewn with lemons, a vase of flowers, a peach seashell shaped object in a bowl.

Inside from the pink rumbles of clouds is a multicolored artist's studio, with paintings, pedestals supporting sculptures, a red floor, a potted plant.

Inside from the curvy branched green tree, villa of dreams, are mustard walls, a dark brick-red wainscot, and two yellow women sitting at an equally dark, brick-red table with a vase of yellow flowers.

Inside from the Avenue des Promenades window is a modern, Coco Chanel, bobbed haired woman, sitting under the window glass, on a paisley divan of indigo, tawny, and burnt orange.

Inside from the palm tree fronds is a table of greenish ochre fruit, and a signature stripe wall of giant crystal shapes in black and yellow and giant leaf shapes in brick and moss.

Inside from the tree and walkway are Matisse himself in violet striped pajamas, standing, looking down on a seated Mme Mattise in a black robe with moss collar, all sunk into a deep deep deep indigo purple wall.

Inside from the deceptively simple child's meadow and white puffy tree leaf bulbs, is a red room, a yellow cat facing you on a purple stool, its paw in the fishbowl, not yet touching the three orange fish, the cat's head down in concentration, eyes on the goldfish, other paw balancing. Behind the yellow cat is the signature stripe wall, red with violet leaf or flowers. On the purple stool, in front of the fishbowl, two oranges and lemon.

Always a Window …

Always a window, always a view to landscape, a fire escape, an inside and outside complementary, inextricable, two sides of the same coin.

Always a window means there is another place, out there. A place in the world. A less private place. Sunny, windy, waving leaves on tree branches, wavy palm fronds, sparkly glints of waves off ocean, shimmery glints of heat off a Moroccan desert village.

There was always a window to look out of, to see the sea, to see the calm, soothing expanse of water; but now the window is there for another purpose. You think, after you die, you will slip through it, and out, into the universe: a universe of pure color, pure shape, pure line – where everything seeks balance.

The Only Blue

Here is your secret: the blue of the Morpho butterfly. Iridescent. Many shades, but metallic, quicksilver, glinty, refracting light. For you it is the only blue that matters, even though you have used so many.

Did you first see the blue in the butterfly at Renoir's house in Cagnes sur Mer? Or, was it in Morocco, on the rough plaster walls, shutters, and wooden gates; powdered – in burlap sacks in shops?

Cerulean sea and aquamarine sky are the boundless spaces you call cosmic. But also stones, minerals – lapis, beryl, topaz, turquoise, tourmaline. What would you say about this blue, now?

Why, amongst the hundreds of shades of blue, amongst all the blues you've used, must there be only one perfect blue?

Acknowledgements

In large part, I owe my writing career to the encouragement and generosity of the Stegner Fellowship at Stanford University, a Fine Arts Work Center Provincetown Fellowship, a National Endowment for the Arts grant, and writer's residencies at: MacDowell, Yaddo, Millay, Montalvo and Djerassi. Paul Nelson has responded faithfully to my manuscripts over thirty years. The University of California Santa Cruz provided an environment where undergraduates were free to be creative, iconoclastic, and challenge traditional ways of thinking. Dr. Frank X. Barron nominated me for a University of California Regents Scholarship and facilitated my spending ten months in Paris France during my senior year at UC Santa Cruz. When I was in my twenties, magazine editors Roger Angell at the *New Yorker*, and Mike Curtis at the *Atlantic*, responded positively to my short stories, which encouraged me in my writing. Novelist Ken Scambray recommended me to Guernica Editions. I must also thank my publishers: Michael Mirolla, Antonio D'Alfonso and Connie McParland; Greg Pece, Leah Maines and Christen Kincaid. I am also grateful for ongoing support from Donna Graboff, Nonnette Sherry, and Bruce Bangert.

This book was written with the assistance of a sabbatical leave from the University of Lynchburg.

Textual Acknowledgements

Herself Surprised – title of the second Joyce Cary novel in *The Horse's Mouth Trilogy*
Room with A View – novel title, E.M. Forster
"Nice is a fishbowl." Dominique Fourcade
"It is necessary to be bored and pull yourself out of boredom." Hardy Hansen, Emeritus Professor of Art, University of California Santa Cruz
Plato: http://www.ilovephilosophy.com/viewtopic.php?f=3&t=187287
"Unless the work is going to save me." HM to son Pierre, 9/12/35
"… creating endlessly; laughter needs an echo …" Henri Bergson
"We are stardust." Joni Mitchell from "We are made of stardust," Shakespeare.

About the Author

Laura Marello is author of novels *Claiming Kin* – finalist for the Paterson Prize in Fiction – *The Tenants of the Hotel Biron, Maniac Drifter, Gauguin's Moon, The Gender of Inanimate Objects* – shortlisted for the Saroyan Prize in Literature – and *Balzac's Robe*. She has been a Stegner Fellow, Fine Arts Work Center Fellow and recipient of the National Endowment for the Arts Grant. She studied poetry with Ray Carver, and Black Mountain poet Edward Dorn, and fiction with Gil Sorrentino and Padma Hejmadi. She is currently working on a novel about San Francisco Architect Julia Morgan.

Printed in May 2022
by Gauvin Press,
Gatineau, Québec